Final Passenger

Final Passenger

Above the Rain Collective
2024

Above the Rain Collective
abovetheraincollective@gmail.com
North Georgia, USA

Contributing Editor: J.A. Sexton

Publisher's note:

ISBN: 979-8-9899186-1-4

abovetheraincollective.com

Cover graphics and interior formatting by J.A. Sexton
Above the Rain logo artwork by Bee Freitag
Original Photo by Ryan McGuire

For all the authors doing the grind

Table of Contents

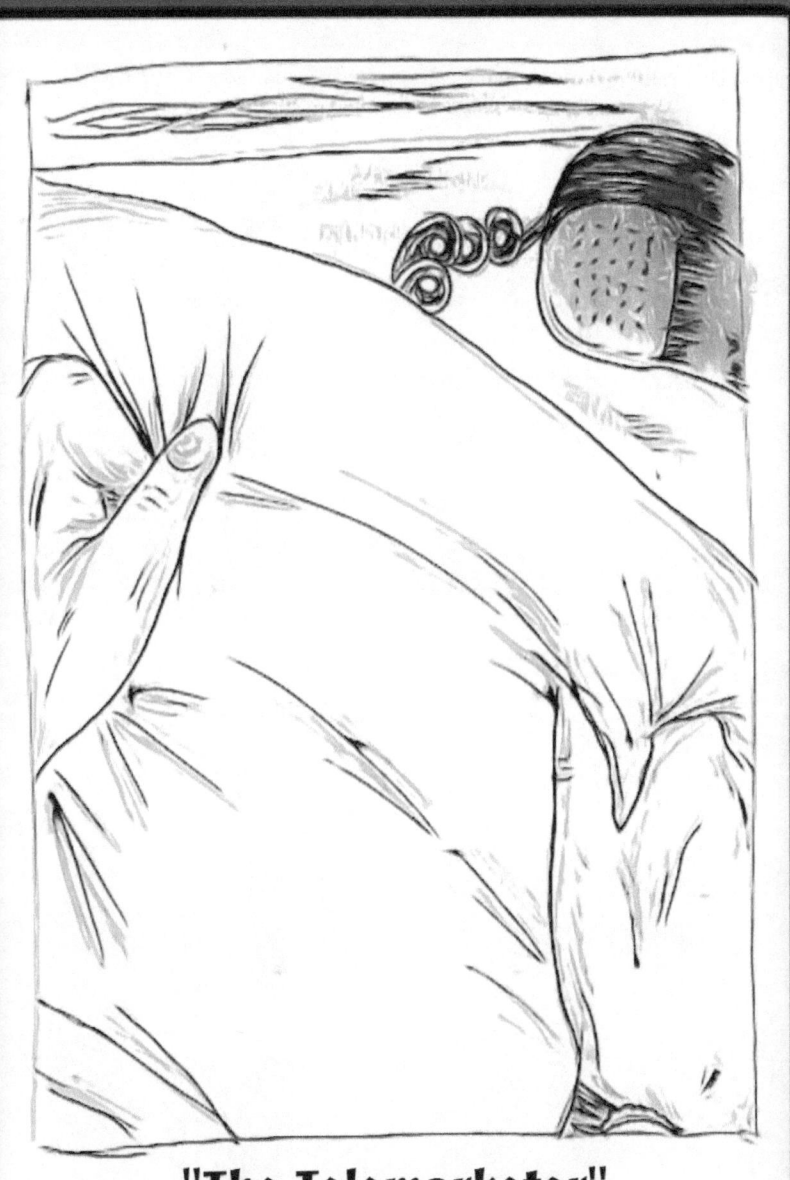

"The Telemarketer"

The Telemarketer

By Mike Trippiedi

A t age forty-five, Nathan Getz was the oldest telemarketer in the company. Most of his co-workers were college kids trying to help pay for schooling and couldn't believe he had done the same meaningless job for most of his adult life.

In a profession that required a lot of phone abuse, Getz was somewhat of a legend among his co-workers. No one could understand his constant positive attitude, nor his uncanny pride at being a member of a profession that most of the country despised.

With its high turnover rate, the company didn't invest much in the telemarketing department. Knowing most of them would be leaving soon, the higher-ups figured it wasn't worth the effort to give their employees any incentive to stay. So at almost twenty years on the job, Nathan Getz was given only a one-week vacation each year. It didn't matter to him.

One week was plenty.

His choice of holiday spots was never anywhere most people would go to get away. Instead of skiing in Colorado, swimming in an ocean on either coast, or the many tourist sights of any major city, he would vacation in places not known for sightseeing or relaxation.

Towns like Fort Wayne, Indiana; Lapeer, Michigan; Sadorus, Illinois; and Ballard, Mississippi were just a few of the places he had visited on previous vacations. This year was no exception. His one-week vacation would be spent in Dalton, Georgia.

Since no flights flew directly into Dalton he had to fly to Atlanta and rent a car. Even though Nathan never showed stress on the job, the drive along Interstate 75 made him aware he was starting to relax. The change of scenery helped, but it was the fact he didn't have to make any phone calls for one week that put an unforeseen grin on his face.

He was also thinking of Christine Wheeler, which made his grin grow into a wide smile. She didn't know he was coming to visit. The last time they spoke, he never let on he would be in Dalton.

This trip would be a surprise.

Nathan Getz was twelve years younger than Christine Wheeler, and while the seasoned telemarketer was somewhat of a loner, Wheeler was the exact opposite. She was outgoing. He was introverted. She was a smoker and a drinker. He was not. She had many friends. He had none.

The only traits shared were the fact they were both single and that neither one of them knew what the other looked like. They had only talked on the phone – the inanimate object that produced so much pain for him. Soon though, his hurt would temporarily vanish while Nathan Getz and Christine Wheeler would finally come face to face.

She was a bartender at a dilapidated downtown tavern called Willie's. What started as a part-time job to get through college, Christine discovered she liked the work, tips, hours, and the customers much more than school. When she dropped out and started bartending full-time, she told herself it was just a short break and she'd be back in school next semester to finish her degree in marketing.

That was twenty years ago. Since then, the closest she had come to anything relating to "promotion" had been her black "Willie's" tee shirt she put on each night before she went to work. Christine Wheeler could have worked at a classier place, but she loved where she was and the regulars loved her back. She had charm, as well as having the knack for mixing a good drink – the perfect combination for success in the bartender trade.

Her charisma was so natural, one never noticed her plain face, and likewise, ordinary body. Nathan didn't know she was a bartender. In their talks, the subject of what profession she had never came up. All he really knew was her address, phone number, the sound of her voice, and what he assumed she was like based on a few phone conversations.

It was late when he arrived at his destination. He found a cheap hotel about twenty miles from Dalton and checked in. He was tired and decided that he would find her in the morning. After all, there was no hurry. He had a whole week.

Nathan shut his eyes for what he thought would be a couple of minutes but soon fell fast asleep, fully clothed, on top of his cheap hotel bed. No dreams. Nightmares. All in one form or another about phone abuse, which was fairly common for a telemarketer.

But he was on vacation, and soon the bad dreams temporarily would stop. They always did when he was away from the phones.

Nathan woke early – before five. He checked the directions on his phone and drove to Christine Wheeler's house. He had no trouble finding the street or her residence. He took a chance she was still asleep. Since he wasn't quite sure how he was going to approach her, he decided to sit in his car and wait for her to leave the house.

The morning passed.

Not one vehicle or person went by as he waited in his car for some sign of life to appear from the Wheeler home. Around noon, the garage door opened and a disheveled-looking woman wearing a torn tee shirt and old sweatpants walked out and started to water the flowers that were to the side of her house.

Having earlier done an image search, he positively identified the woman in front of the house as Christine Wheeler.

"Now my vacation begins," he said to the dashboard.

Irrational thoughts popped into his mind. He wondered if she had been with a guy last night, and if so, was he inside her house right now, perhaps taking a shower or cooking her breakfast or lunch?

"Don't do this," he said aloud as he stopped himself from punching the steering wheel. "Now is not the time to act erratic."

The woman finished watering the flowers and closed the garage door as she went inside. Assuming she would shower and change clothes before she left the house, Nathan decided to take a break and get a bite to eat.

He returned forty minutes later.

Another hour passed.

The garage door opened again. This time she was in her car. He watched her back out of the driveway and drive off. After starting the ignition of his rented car, he quickly followed her.

Her first stop was a shopping mall. She purchased some shoes in one store, candles in another, and several greeting cards in a third. She paid for everything with cash.

Leaving the mall, she drove a few blocks to a gas station where she proceeded to fill her car with unleaded. Next, a fast-food drive-thru. From there, she drove a couple of miles to Willie's Tavern. The perfect setting to finally talk face to face, he thought, as he watched her stroll into the bar.

After waiting a couple of minutes, he took a deep breath and cautiously walked up to the tavern door. *Act natural,* he coached himself, before entering the friendly-looking pub.

It was quiet inside. Too quiet for his comfort, but he figured the place would fill up when the average workday ended, which would be soon. There were two business types in a booth by the window, an old man sitting alone at the bar, and Christine Wheeler, the lone female, putting money in the jukebox.

Nathan could feel his nerves taking control, so he went directly to the restroom to calm himself down. He looked in

7

the mirror and smiled at his reflection, knowing at that moment his trip to Georgia was the right thing to do.

When he returned, he was shocked to see the woman he had traveled so far to meet was actually the bartender.

"What's your poison?" she said with a smile.

"What?"

"What would you like to drink?"

"Oh, I'm sorry. Soda."

"Big spender," she said, turning to prepare the simplest drink in her repertoire.

Nathan awkwardly propped himself up on the barstool. Timidly he asked, "Can I sit here?"

"You don't come to bars much, do you?"

"No."

"What brings you to this one?"

Don't you recognize my voice?, he thought, but all he got out was, "I'm just passing through."

"Well, enjoy your stay. Holler when you're dry. I'm Christine."

I know, he wanted to say, but settled with, "Nice to meet you."

She left to pour another beer for the old man sitting at the other end of the bar, and when she returned to Nathan, he was gone, replaced by a ten-dollar bill sitting next to his empty soda glass.

"Looks like it's going to be a good night," she said to herself as she rang up the dollar drink and pocketed the remaining nine. Nathan's face was already out of her memory, and his voice, the one thing people remembered most about him, was long forgotten.

Christine Wheeler's shift ended as usual. The owner, Joey Vincennes, helped her to close the tavern, and like he'd done hundreds of times before, walked her to her car in the empty parking lot to make sure she drove away safely. He waved as her car drove out of the lot, not having any idea that the man who left the biggest tip of the evening was hiding in her back seat.

Nathan had been still for hours, and now that Christine was finally in her car, he knew one little sound would ruin everything. He stayed motionless, hiding on the floor directly behind her, hoping his legs wouldn't cramp.

With the car radio blaring and the off-duty bartender singing loudly off-key, Nathan was able to adjust his body position from time to time without any hint of an uninvited guest being detected.

To Nathan, the ten-minute drive to Christine's house felt like twenty. He wanted to take his plastic gloves off and air out his perspiring hands, or sit up and stretch his back, but he knew the destination was soon approaching. Instead, he focused his thoughts on the real reason he was in Dalton, which helped ease the anxiety of the moment.

A sigh of relief fell upon him as he heard Christine Wheeler's garage door begin to open. He was motionless as she pulled into her driveway. He heard the car engine shut off, felt her leave the front seat, and grimaced as she slammed the car door. He was now the sole occupant of her car, as well as finally being all alone in her garage.

Nathan silently recited the alphabet fifty times before he cautiously sat up in the back seat. Realizing he was alone,

Nathan then set the alarm on his watch and lay down in the back seat of Christine's car to get some sleep.

Two hours later, the alarm on Nathan's watch went off. He got out of the car and gently shut the door. He then, very softly, walked into the home of Christine Wheeler. With help from his pocket flashlight, Nathan was able to stumble onto some cookies he found in the cabinet.

After sitting down on her couch and quietly eating in the dark, Nathan was now ready to find the bedroom where he knew the bartender was sleeping.

It was easy to find her. All he had to do was follow the sound of the loud snoring. He stood next to the bed and stared emotionlessly at her while she slept. As he watched, all of the previous phone calls he'd had with her over the past year came back with clarity.

Soon, his mind wandered to the other people he'd visited on his previous vacations. Rowena Hurt from Fort Wayne. Carl Musser – Lapeer. Donald Drake – Sadorus, and Deanna Thompson from Ballard, plus so many more. Now it was Christine Wheeler's turn to join the list and to pay the price for being disrespectful.

"I was just trying to do my job," Nathan said, as he picked up the pillow next to her sleeping head. "You have no idea the kind of cruelty my phone calls provoke. Cause if you did, you would never have said all those hurtful things to me. Me! An average guy, just trying to make ends meet!"

Christine's snoring stopped. Her eyes blinked open, but the pillow in Nathan's hands covered her face before her brain waves reached her mouth to form a scream. Her arms and legs instinctively fought as the vacationing telemarketer leaned forward with all of his weight, speaking through the pillow that was quickly obstructing her breathing.

"All you had to say was you weren't interested, or that you couldn't afford anything at this time. I'd have understood. Or better yet, why didn't you just hang up? No. You had to make hurtful comments. And you just kept digging into me. Of all the people I called this past year, you were by far the worst! I'm a person too, Christine Wheeler! You vulgar, bad-mannered, discourteous slob!"

Her body jerked as it struggled for life, and the more she flailed, the stronger Nathan became.

"I'm sorry if my calls interrupted your dinner, or your nap, or your favorite program, but you see, I'm nothing more than a person trying to survive. Like you at this very moment."

Christine had a lot of fight in her, but she was quickly losing the battle as the pillow the overwrought intruder held tightly over her face continued to block the air going to and from her nose and mouth.

On any given day, she probably could have beaten Nathan at arm wrestling, but she was blindsided by this attack. The fact it was fueled with pent-up rage, gave him the edge.

And the kill.

Nathan watched as her body went from struggle to calm, life to death. Once he was sure she was gone, he slowly lifted the pillow off the dead woman's face, revealing wide-open eyes and a thick line of white discharge that trailed from her mouth to the pillow.

"Vacation over so soon?" he asked himself. "And I was just starting to have some fun."

***

Nathan Getz spent a few days driving through the state of Georgia before traveling home to resume his job as a telemarketer. He would go back to his work happy, knowing he had continued to make his profession easier – one person at a time. Where will his vacation take him next year?

That all depends on the people he calls.

Mike Trippiedi is a former filmmaker who found it a lot cheaper to turn his many inspirations into short stories and novels. He is currently working on his third novel, a historical fiction / political satire, called "Abraham Lincoln's Traveling Medicine Show."

In addition to writer, Mike has worn many hats in his lifetime. Including telemarketer.

"Mister"

Mister

By Kirsten Noelle Craig

Ari checked her reflection in the visor mirror before closing it up and glancing over to the driver's seat. Her sister Kieran was staring intently at her phone screen, her posture screaming frustration.

She must have felt eyes studying her because she asked, "What?" without lifting her eyes from her screen.

"Nothin'. Just wondering what we're doing." Ari drew the reply out in a bored, singsong drawl she knew would irritate her sister.

Kieran didn't take the bait. She sighed and lowered her phone to her lap. "We are waiting for Dez to get here and then we are headed out. It's not fully dark anyway, so. No harm in hanging out a bit longer."

Ari hummed in acknowledgment and pulled the visor down to check her face again.

Half an hour later, the girls were driving down Highway 411 with their friend Desiree in tow. Kieran had the windows rolled down halfway, so the heady summer scent of wet grass and cooling asphalt flooded into the car.

Desiree wasted no time in taking up her favorite pastime of sharing all the local gossip with the sisters. In a town like the one they called home, that gossip sometimes amounted to someone's cow getting loose and blocking Clear Creek Road for two hours. Ari nodded and gasped at the appropriate times in the one-sided conversation.

Kieran gripped the steering wheel tighter than necessary and kept her eyes fixed on the dark road ahead of them.

As the car turned slowly onto the unpaved, potholed road of their destination, Ari cleared her throat. "So, what's the plan for tonight?"

The question was aimed at her sister. She knew Kieran was upset and wanted to shake her free from her thoughts by focusing on their goals for this adventure. In their town, summer entertainment for young people was limited. The three of them had started a tradition of ghost hunting two summers ago and they took it seriously.

The town might lack any kind of store other than a solitary gas station, but it did not disappoint when it came to cemeteries or creepy locations.

"I had planned for the usual, Ari. Get there and look around. See what we can see. Go from there." Kieran delivered these goals with zero excitement and Ari wondered why she had even agreed to come out tonight if she wasn't feeling it.

With the attempt to snap her sister out of her funk a failure, Ari decided not to push it any further. They could do this one cemetery exploration and go home.

"I can't believe we haven't come to this one before, you guys! Everyone is always talkin' about how scary and cursed it is." Dez was practically bouncing in the backseat as she thought about being able to tell her other friends she had visited the abandoned cemetery. "This is gonna be so crazy!"

The cemetery was one they had to look hard to find when driving down the perilous backroads. It was called the abandoned cemetery by locals because its history was all but forgotten. The headstones dated from before the 1900s and no one knew who was buried there. Some of the grave markers were just moss-covered rocks, carefully placed by mourners of the past. The graves even continued back into the dense forest of trees as if nature decided it was done sharing space with humans.

There was a rough entrance to the cemetery made by nothing but other cars pulling into it. Kieran guided the car into the small space and killed the ignition. She glanced down at her phone with eyebrows creased. Whatever she found on the screen must not have been to her liking because she popped open the glove compartment and shoved her cell into it. Ari and Dez were already standing near the front of the car, so she locked up and headed to join them.

After several moments of shifting awkwardly from foot to foot, Ari spoke up. "Kieran? What do you want to do first?" She tried to keep her tone calm and gentle.

Her sister's mood had only seemed to darken since arriving at the cemetery. Ari wasn't used to overseeing expeditions and out of lifelong conditioning she relied heavily on her older sister's direction.

Kieran shook her head as if warding off thoughts she didn't want in her head before replying, "Right. Um, we could start down that path over there that runs parallel to the graves? See what we feel?"

The plan seemed solid enough for the other two and the girls started walking toward the path Kieran pointed out. Light filtered down into the cemetery from the almost full moon above them. Crickets droned their nighttime songs further off into the forest.

It had been a hotter-than-usual summer and the humidity of the air felt like a heavy cloak mixing with the stillness of the cemetery. Ari followed Kieran dutifully down the path. She was grateful for the moon tonight because she forgot to grab the flashlight from the car.

Ari grunted and stumbled but managed to right herself without falling. She called over her shoulder, "Be careful where you put your feet. There's a lot of roots jutting out over here."

As soon as the words left Ari's mouth, Dez yelled out from behind them. The sisters turned to find her sprawled out on her stomach across the path. She screamed again and reached her hand around to her right calf. "My leg! Damnit, that hurts!"

Ari felt panic start to build in her chest. She hated blood and didn't think there was a first aid kit in the car. Her mind cycled through what she remembered from middle school summer camp about how to care for sprains and breaks. Nothing helpful solidified in her mind.

Dez continued to moan from the ground.

Pushing away the panic, Ari knelt next to Dez and tried to soothe her hollering. "You're okay, you're okay. Where does it hurt the most? Twisted your ankle?"

Dez forced out ragged words between sobs, "No. My ankle... is fine. It's... my calf."

Ari delicately rolled up Dez's pant leg to try and assess how bad the injury was. What she found on her calf was not the thorn punctures or branch gash she expected. Three deep scratches traveled down the center of the girl's calf. It looked for all the world like a mountain lion had reached out from behind and swiped at her violently.

Ari sputtered, "Wha... I don't... Kieran?" She glanced up to meet her sister's eyes. She hoped for some more support or ideas on what to do.

All Kieran mumbled was, "That doesn't make sense."

Dez choked back her anguished crying long enough to ask. "What? What doesn't make sense?" Her body trembled, and Ari wrapped an arm around her shoulders to comfort the hurt girl.

"Her pants aren't ripped at all. Scratches like those... would rip clean through the pants. It doesn't make sense." A chill climbed up Ari's spine as she realized the sounds of crickets and other woodland murmuration had stopped.

Ari decided it was time to call it quits on this endeavor. Dez's injury looked worse than something they could patch up there in the cemetery. She uncharacteristically gave her sister rapid-fire commands to make sure her friend got help. "Kieran. Get your phone out of the car and call Dez's dad. He will have more first aid supplies and be able to help her better than we can."

Kieran hesitated briefly before nodding in agreement and standing to leave.

"Hurry. Please?" Ari added. Her stomach was turning with an unknown dread. The sooner they got out of this place, the better.

***

Jogging up to her passenger door, Kieran fumbled with the key fob. Her focus was shaky at best, but she finally got the door unlocked and grabbed her phone from the glove compartment. She swiped through the home screen, intending to pull up Dez's dad's number. A recent text notification caught her eye.

"Cool. Look if you're gonna ghost me to walk around in the dark the least you could do is get a picture of the Mister's grave."

Kieran groaned. Of course, Zach would only care about some morbidly famous marker located deep in the cemetery. The marker was notorious because it was crudely shaped like a skull and had only the words "Mister" on it.

The gravestone sat off by itself at the furthest edge of the cemetery. No one knew who or what "Mister" could be, but most speculated it wasn't anything good.

Tossing her keys onto the passenger seat where she wouldn't forget them, Kieran oriented herself to the gravestones spread out before her. She jogged off in the direction she thought the headstone stood. She hoped this act of bravery on her part would patch things up with Zach. Her sister and Dez would be fine for five extra minutes.

Somewhere in the woods, a shadow watched. The light illuminating the path dimmed as a cloud slid in front of the moon. A few feet from where the girls sat huddled together a branch snapped.

"Shit. Okay, we are walking back to the car now. Forget this." Some part of Ari's brain was ringing an alarm and urging her to move. She didn't need any further motivation. She helped Dez stand and coaxed her to lean as much of her weight as she could against her.

Stepping cautiously and clumsily respectively, the girls pointed themselves in the direction of the car. Another branch snapped to their left, but both decided to ignore it.

"Screw this place," Ari said under her breath and picked up her pace. At the head of the trail, a shape came into view in front of them.

"Kieran?" Ari called out with more confidence than she felt. Dez winced as she tried to put her hurt leg down to test her balance. Kieran stepped into view and stooped to take up the role of supporting Dez's weight so Ari could rest.

"Thanks. Did you call her dad?" Ari was too freaked out to stand still in this spot. Adrenaline carried her the last few steps to the car.

"Yeah. He wouldn't get here fast enough so we can just drop her off ourselves," came her sister's monotone response.

Ari quickly opened the back door and helped Kieran situate Dez inside. Kieran's movements seemed jerky and uncoordinated, almost like she was drunk. Dez inhaled sharply as her leg brushed the door's frame. Not wanting to spend another second standing out in the open, Ari picked up the car keys from the passenger seat and slid in. She cranked the car for Kieran who was moving way too slow for her liking.

What is her deal? she thought to herself. This felt like more than just relationship drama.

Kieran backed down the short path they had parked in and swung the car around to face the way they came in. Ari already felt her heart rate slowing and her muscles relaxing as they drove. Remembering Dez was still in pain, she dug around in her bag until her hand found a bottle of pain relievers. She shook a couple out into her palm and passed them back to her.

"You'll be home soon, girl. I'm so sorry this happened."

Dez moaned weakly and swallowed the pills dry.

The car bumped over the last few potholes, and they pulled out onto the main road. They hadn't even been at the cemetery for an hour, but Ari felt like she had run a marathon. She slumped back against the seat. All the excitement and comradery of before had dissipated. Ari doubted there would be any more ghost hunting this summer. She figured it was just as well. She was getting too old to be trampling out in the dark at midnight.

A text chimed on her phone, and she pulled it from her pocket to check it. Confusion washed over her when she read who the text was from. *Kieran.* She glanced briefly at her sister in the driver's seat before opening the text message.

"What the hell, Ari! Why did y'all leave me here?!"

Ari couldn't tear her eyes away from the screen. Her palms started to sweat, and she had to steady her breathing before she gathered enough courage to confront her sister.

"This isn't funny, Kieran. I don't know how you're doing this, but I can't handle it right now. Grow up." She brandished the phone toward her sister to further emphasize how messed up it was. "Dez is hurt, and I feel like I'm gonna have a nervous breakdown. This entire trip you've been sulking. All you're worried about is stupid Zach and what he thinks. Did you ever stop to think about how I'm feeling?! Dez is bleeding right now and you're trying to prank me!!"

Hot tears spilled down her cheeks as the rage choked off her words. She kept looking at her sister's profile, hoping she would say something, anything.

Ari's phone chimed with another text alert. She peered down at the screen. It was Kieran again. "For real. Please come back and get me. I'm scared." Her sister dropped a pin with her location directly after that.

"The cemetery?" Ari couldn't breathe. Her seat belt was pinning her down and the highway sped by in a blur past the windows. She didn't want to look over. She couldn't. Whoever or whatever was driving the car laughed bitterly. Ari felt her face turn toward the sound against her will.

A mangled grey face peered back at her, its black eyes sunken into its head and jagged, brown teeth forming a dangerous grin. Ari screamed and flailed violently trying to unbuckle her seatbelt. Somehow in her head, climbing into the backseat with Dez would be safer than staying up here with whatever this was.

The seatbelt was stuck fast. She slammed her body against the passenger door to put as much space between her and this demon as possible. It continued laughing. The sound wormed its way into Ari's thoughts, and she clamped her hands over her ears to muffle it.

"Where's my sister?!?" she screamed over the deranged laughing.

The question was purely rhetorical because she knew where Kieran was. A better question would have been, "How?" She rocked back and forth hoping she could rock herself awake from this nightmare. Mercifully, the thing driving her sister's car grew quiet.

She whispered this time, "Where is Kieran?" Ari's blood froze in her veins as the thing answered her.

"Your sister is with the Mister now." It jerked the wheel of the car and it careened sickeningly toward a tree. Ari prayed she would lose consciousness before impact.

Kirsten has held a lifelong fascination with the weird, unseen corners of the universe. She wrote this story in between downing cups of coffee and reading way too many books at one time. She is currently pursuing her Bachelors in Library and Information Sciences.

Kirsten lives in Chattanooga, Tennessee with her kiddos, 3 cats, and 10 backyard chickens.

You can follow her on any social media platform with the handle @ TheSpineOfMotherhood

"Skitter"

Skitter

By Pete Russo

T he dead woman stared at the floor, face largely obscured by the bill of a baseball cap neatly pulled down for this express purpose. Instead of feeling relieved, however, Harold feared it would only take one particularly impactful jolt of the train car to reveal what happened.

Skitter skitter skitter.

To make matters worse, Zed thought it was hilarious.

"Stop laughing," said Harold.

"You warned her," retorted Zed.

"You didn't need to kill her!"

"There you go, blaming me for your problems. This is how you got into this mess, remember?"

They sat next to each other, and despite the fact that they were speeding through an underground tunnel, Harold was sure that someone was behind him, looking at him through the window.

Skitter skitter skitter.

"This is bad," said Harold, standing up and pacing a sloppy line. "I'm sweating. Look at me, Zed - I'm wearing my nicest suit and I'm getting sweat stains all over it."

"Will you just calm down?" asked Zed, the impatience all over his voice. "It's a nice enough ride, and all your troubles are almost over anyway. Another few hours and there'll be a whole slate of new problems to worry about."

Skitter skitter skitter.

The sweat, the anxiety, and the dead body were bad enough, but that skittering sound was over the top. It reminded Harold of a tap dancer on a pane of glass. He could see the dancer in his mind's eye, perched on the edge of his seat, the anxiety raising the hair on the back of his neck. Every second, he was expecting to see the glass break, and every second that it didn't, the inevitable just felt worse.

"You did it," reminded Harold. He glared at Zed, who looked unconcerned.

"In the long run, it's better this way."

"For who?" asked Harold. "For you?" He pointed at the hunched-over body. "For her?" The third question, "For me?"' died on his lips before it could be asked.

"With her gone, there's no questions," replied Zed.

"Nobody to say, 'Hey, what's in that jar?' or, 'Hey, why you sweating in the middle of winter?' or, 'Who you talking to?'"

Harold glared at Zed and looked away - out the pane of glass and into the dark tunnel.

"You know I'm right."

Skitter skitter skitter.

"You didn't need to kill her," repeated Harold.

"All we needed was for her to get a good look at us," reminded Zed. "Ask the wrong questions, recognize the logo on the jar, and it's all over."

The jar.

Harold looked at the floor in front of the woman, slumped over in her seat. Shards of glass surrounded her feet, with the largest piece still bearing a tightly screwed-on, sealed lid with the "CHEMBIO" logo stamped on the top. Immediately, Harold dropped to his knees and began picking up the shards, flipping the lid over to safely store them.

"Hey," said Zed, tapping him on the hand. Harold ignored him.

"Hey!" repeated Zed, pinching him hard on the forearm.

Harold brushed him off and continued working. Finally, Zed slapped him hard on the neck, and that finally drew Harold's attention. "One way or another, they're gonna find out," he said. "You're wasting time that you could be using to figure out how to get outta here."

Harold shook his head and continued to brush Zed's touch off his arms. "I don't want to get outta here," he insisted. "I know what happened, I know they're going to blame me and they won't believe me when I tell them it was you, but at least I can save the company. Maybe."

More laughter. Zed sat down next to the dead woman and put his feet up on the opposite seat. "Company man to the end, hmmm?" He put an arm around the dead woman and leaned on her shoulder. "What do you think, sweetie? Is this a little much?"

Harold glared at him. "Listen, asshole—"

"What a fool," said the dead woman. She stared at him with contempt in her eyes. "You know you did alla this, right? You read the reports. You put the pieces together. You smuggled the jar outta the lab and you killed me. And now you're still the company man, ready to get your ass beat and tossed in a cell, just to protect the company."

His breath quickened and he fell backward onto the floor. The shards of glass (or was it Zed?) behind him stung as he landed, looking with disbelief into her eyes.

"But... but he killed you," said Harold, pointing at Zed.

"You killed me," shot back the woman as Zed kissed her on the cheek.

"I didn't!"

"Who did, then?" asked Zed. "Me? Did I swing the jar against her face and break both of them at the same time? Do I even have that capacity?"

Harold pulled himself to his feet. He still felt light-headed and unsteady and held onto the closest seat to keep himself upright. "Your plan," he repeated. "Your goals. You wanted it."

"I can't deny that," admitted Zed, holding the woman's hand tightly in his. "But in the end, it was you who did it."

"It's your fault," insisted Harold, though he sounded less sure. He looked out the window, dreading the inevitable next-station-stop.

"Isn't that why you're in this mess?" asked Zed, suddenly right in front of him. "Always blaming someone else for your weaknesses and your mistakes. Maybe if you'd ever taken a stand on something in your entire pitiful life, you wouldn't be here now, hmm?"

"Your fault," repeated Harold, sounding more confused than ever, with sweat pouring down his face. "You killed her. Not me, you. Not me."

Zed sighed. "Maybe," he replied. "Maybe not, but it sure was fun."

That did it. Harold glared at Zed and fired a fist straight into the middle of his face.

THWACK!

Pain reverberated from his knuckles, down the back of his hand, and up his arm, as Harold made contact with the plexiglass window full force.

Behind him, Zed let loose a full belly laugh. "My guy," said Zed. "You're still not catching up with the reality of the situation."

He moved all around Harold, making the latter's eyes start to dance around, and he had to grip the seat with both hands to avoid tipping forward. "Look at yourself," continued Zed.

Easier said than done. The window reflected the harsh fluorescent light from the ceiling of the train car, but the waning sun outside made it a poor mirror. Still, Harold looked. The lights washed him out a decent amount, but he could still note the reddening circles around his eyes that his pale and clammy skin seemed to deepen. Sweat stains had darkened his collar and armpits for hours now, and it was only because his sense of smell seemed to have stopped working that he could not detect the odor of fear that emanated from his body.

And the jitters.

Skitter skitter skitter.

And the anxiety.

"I just need to get home," said Harold, to nobody in particular. "If I can get home, I can take care of this."

"Well..." said Zed, as his own eyes drifted outside.

Harold closed his in response. He could feel the train slowing down and didn't need to look out the window to see the station approaching.

"Maybe it'll just be a few people," he said. "Maybe they'll avoid this car."

"Maybe you should've waited for the express," countered Zed. "Still two more stops to go before you get to what you think is safety."

The train pulled to a stop, and Harold felt his pulse quicken. It caused him a moment of concern when it was strongest behind his eyes, but he ignored the dark spots in his vision as he rushed to the door just as it opened.

"Sorry, car closed," he said, in the face of a surprised teenager. "Go to the next."

Perhaps it was the sudden surprise at his outburst, but the small gathering that was about to enter Harold's train car stopped in their tracks and turned to the next. A wave of relief washed over his face as he let out the breath he had been holding.

It didn't last.

"Great," said Zed. "So much for not drawing attention to yourself. But there's two entrances to this car." He gestured behind Harold, who watched in horror as the door on the opposite end opened, and a completely new set of afternoon commuters streamed in. Far too many to cut off at this point.

"Better run, rabbit," taunted Zed.

Mind racing, Harold did the math. He felt the train begin to move again under his feet and the realization rapidly smacks him in the face with two words flashing before his eyes.

TOO LATE.

Skitter skitter skitter.

With surprising swiftness, Harold braced himself on both rows of seats as he scampered down the aisle to the dead woman, landing next to her before the new arrivals had the chance to see her current state. She had stopped talking and looked as lifeless as she had since he saw her take her last breath. Subtly adjusting her hat to cover the wound on the top and side of her head, Harold did his best to act natural.

"Hey," said Zed, from directly behind him. "You think they'll notice?"

"Quiet," replied Harold, between gritted teeth.

"You think they'll walk past and see you, assume you're tweaking on something and she's overdosed?"

"Shut. Up," said Harold, more insistently.

"At this point, it's hard to determine which would be worse, right?"

Ignoring the incessant whisper behind his head, Harold managed to sit still for several seconds, his eyes darting around their sockets, gratefully taking in the fact that nobody was sitting near him.

"Tickets, tickets please," said the conductor from somewhere behind him. Not even this was cause for concern; he'd shown his ticket when he first boarded, as did the dead woman next to him.

Click click click click click.

Unfortunately, this fact didn't stop the rapid fire of the ticket puncher from hammering in his head, several times louder than it had any cause to be.

"Tickets, tickets please."

Click click click click click.

Skitter skitter skitter.

"You don't look so good," said Zed. "You need a drink?"

A drop of sweat rolled down the side of Harold's face, and he wiped it with one shaking hand, determined to maintain his composure.

"Or something to eat," continued Zed. "You're really pale. I'm sure there's at least one good samaritan on this train with some cookies or juice."

Skitter skitter skitter.

"Shut your goddamn mouth."

Click click click click click.

"Now take her for example," said Zed, pointing at the dead woman. "She doesn't look like she's missed too many meals." He smiled, though at this point Harold thought it looked more like an evil leer. "Just go through her bag, man. It's not like she's gonna complain."

"Tickets, tickets please."

"WILL YOU SHUT YOUR FUCKING TRAP YOU ASSHOLE!" Mortified, Harold slowly looked around the now-silent train car, with the only noise being that of the wheels on the track. The rest of the car was staring at him, their typical afternoon commute broken up by the confusion of the sudden outburst.

Some mouths were agape. Some had fear in their eyes. Two rows behind him, the conductor reached for Harold. "Calm down, sir. Everything–"

Harold pulled away before the conductor could reach him. "Stay back," he warned.

Skitter skitter skitter.

He turned his head. Zed was standing amongst the crowd, hand over his mouth in an exaggerated, silent laugh. In front of him, a single man stepped forward.

"Ma'am, are you all right? Ma–"

The pit in Harold's stomach dropped another few feet as he realized that the conductor was speaking to the dead woman. Zed's eyes widened in faux-shock as the conductor reached toward–

"No, leave her alone!" Still unsteady, Harold lunged forward to push the conductor away, but he lost his balance and fell into the opposite seat just in time to see her fall over, eyes open and glazed.

The blood from her ear had dried and caked by now, but it was clear, what it was, to all who could see.

"Oh my word, she's dead," said the conductor, loud enough for everyone to hear.

Skitter skitter skitter.

Confusion turned to shock turned to fear as a gun was drawn. Behind the man with the gun, Zed continued to silently laugh, his body shaking from holding in the sound.

"On your knees, hands in the air," said the man, his voice as steady as his aim. "Police."

The crowd took as big of a step away from him as they were able, and the conductor dove into a side seat out of the line of fire as the gun came out, though there was a palpable sense of relief at the word 'police'.

Except for Zed. He stepped forward, right behind the man with the gun.

"No," said Harold.

"I won't ask again," came the reply.

"Don't do this," said Harold. "Not to someone else."

A smile grew on Zed's face as he tapped the officer on the neck. He barely reacted, brushing at his neck with one hand while never letting the gun waver.

"Last chance," said the officer, "On your knees, hands in the air."

Harold locked eyes with Zed. The latter leaned in and whispered into the officer's ear, which was all the provocation needed.

"NO!" shouted Harold, rushing the officer, who instinctively opened fire.

***

"ID says Harold Lawson, worked for Chembio," said the officer to the paramedic just outside the stopped train. "Witnesses say he was acting squirrely since he got on, so we'll need to see the tox screen once it's available."

"That's obvious, Hank," replied the medic. "Between you and me, I don't trust that place. Private security has it locked down tight as hell, but I heard there's always a biohazard truck going in or out of it. Creepy." He gestured at the second covered gurney. "What about her?"

Hank shook his head.

"No idea, Pete," he said. "Witnesses say she wasn't moving the entire time they were there, so she was likely already dead."

Pete slowly nodded while looking over his clipboard. "My preliminary guess was that the blunt force trauma to the head was enough to cause death, but we'll give a once over as well."

"Great," replied Hank, offering his hand to shake. "I'm just glad I was there to help when I could. Anything to worry about from the passengers?"

"Nah," said Pete. "Some hysteria, but nobody else was hurt. We spent more time treating a few insect bites than we did any legit injuries." He cocked his head and pointed at Hank's neck. "That itch? Mix up some water and baking soda and wash it out, should be good as new."

Hank felt the slightly raised, slightly irritated bump on his neck. "Honestly, it was actually nice to get a little reminder'a summer, yeah?"

"Hah! You got that right. Alright, my friend - I'll get those autopsy reports over as soon as they're ready."

The two men shook hands and parted ways. Pete walked back toward the flashing lights, while Hank checked the time and started to calculate the best way for him to make the rest of his trip home.

"That was close."

It was enough to make him flinch, if not jump. Henry Fleur had nine years on the force and wasn't one to scare easily, but there was nobody around him that he could see, and the sudden voice seemingly from out of nowhere was enough to give anyone pause.

"What?" he asked the night air.

"Harold didn't have the stones to follow through with what he had to do. But I know you do. Don't'cha, Hank?"

Follow through.

What was he doing on that train?

What did he have to do?

"Who are you?" he asked. "Where are you?"

"You can finish the story, right, Hank? You can go down in history."

"What story?" asked Hank. "Finish what? What......"

"..."

"What do I need to do?"

"We'll get to that," replied Zed. "But for right now?" He smiled. "Where do you live?"

Skitter skitter.

Pete Russo has been writing short stories, long stories, and poetry since the age of fifteen. His previously published novel, One Chance: The Legend of Valerian's Garden is available on Amazon. He lives in Savannah, GA, and to the best of his knowledge, has never been involved in an incident on a train.

"I'm Not Sorry"

I'm Not Sorry

By Juliet Rose

The streaks still run down the wall
Where you threw a glass of water at me
Outlasting your presence in my life

The kitchen window remains shattered
When you punched your fist about dirty dishes
Reminiscent of your unending anger

The wall in the bedroom is still damaged
From how you slammed my head against it
When I dared to disagree with you

The scars still mar my body and mind
Left by your unrelenting rage over nothing
Slowly healing in your absence

Your body rots deep in the ground

Where I placed it in the dark of night
After I finally snapped from your abuse

Your memory is fading day by day
Releasing me from your cruel grip
Breath returning to my battered body

The final ride we took together that night
Reminding me of the first time we rode
The future seeming bright and beautiful.

This time, though, the ride was my freedom
Your body silent and no longer hateful
I am at peace, even if you aren't

For that, I am not sorry.

Juliet Rose is a multi-award-winning cross-genre author in contemporary fiction, visionary suspense, sci-fi realism, and supernatural horror. She is adept at blending genres and challenges both herself and the reader to think outside of their comfort zone by introducing new ideas into familiar tropes. She has ten published fiction books. In her free time, she also dabbles in magazine and anthology writing. While she resides in the mountains of Georgia, she's lived all over the United States and Mexico, using these experiences in her writing.

Her website is authorjulietrose.com and includes all of her social media links and contacts.

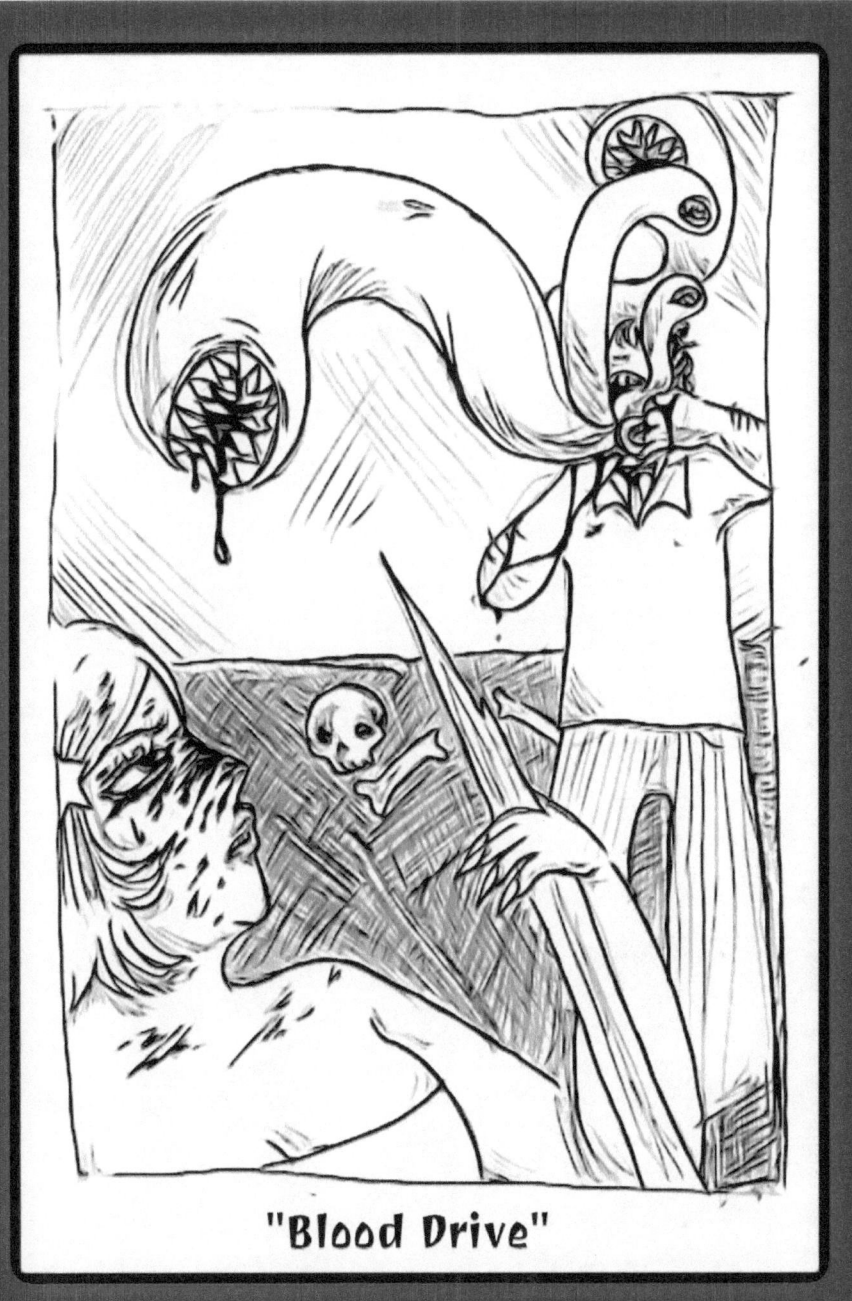

"Blood Drive"

Blood Drive

By Jacob Anderer

It's a beautiful night. The moon is full and bright, the stars are sparkling above, and the breeze is just right. I glance at my phone to see 12:07 am, the Uber notification says Javi will be here at 12:45 am. Time to kick off the make-up and get ready.

Tonight I'm going to a party, and I need to look somewhat presentable. I run my fingers through my hair, combing some knots out, and apply blush and highlight to my cheeks. I'm a sucker for a glow-in-the-dark star, so I slap one on my hip and finish off with a coat of lip gloss.

The front door of the complex is broken, so I head out the door and down the stairs to the basement. It's always the same down here when there are better things going on around town, empty and cold.

Normally, a bunch of us hang out in the basement after work, drink and play music. There are couches and pool tables for lounging, and an old bar for drinking.

It's a nice place to be in the middle of the week when plans are limited. The only downside is the lack of sunlight, thanks to there being no windows. The only real light we get down here is from the exit sign above the only way in and out of this complex.

As I wait for my ride, I perch on the stair rails for a moment and watch the door to the apartment building across the street. It opens and closes rhythmically, like a metronome. I wonder who lives in that apartment. I wonder what kind of person I am going to meet tonight. I wonder what kind of person I am. The moment I think these thoughts, a hand reaches out and pins me against the wall. I scream and try to fight my way out, but the grip is too strong.

"Woah, woah, woah, relax, Mel, it's me! Don't break my nose over a shitty prank!" said the man as he loosened his grip and let me go.

I turned and came face to face with my shitbag friend Carter, backing away with his hands up in a defensive position. Just behind him was Talia, cackling away like a hyena.

I laughed, too, once I realized that I was no longer in danger. "You're both pricks," I said as I went to push Carter playfully, but not too playfully because I was still kind of pissed. He didn't budge an inch. Carter is built like a brick shithouse, what did I think my scrawny ass push was going to do?

"You love us," Talia slipped in between dying cackles, "How much longer on that Uber?"

I checked my phone. "Uhmm, it says Javi should be here now, be on the lookout for a black Cadillac Escalade."

Just then came a loud, but quick, honk from just up the street. The Escalade tore down the street at what seemed like a Mach 10 pace, probably not wanting to be late and risk getting a one-star review. He came to a screeching stop directly in front of us, and according to my phone, it was 12:45 am. He was right on time.

click click

All the doors unlocked and before we all got into this stranger's car, I stuck my head in and asked, "You're Javi, right?"

"Yes, that is me. I am Javi, and you must be Mel and friends?" Javi responded in a smooth, almost radio show host voice. It was kind of soothing, but somehow out of place.

"Yep, that's us! Now let's get this shit started, we have a party to get to," Carter said as he threw himself into the car and slung the seatbelt over his chest.

Once we were all in and buckled up, Javi pulled away, and on we went toward our destination. The car itself was very clean, almost spotless, which isn't weird, but at the same time, I wondered how he managed to keep it so fresh after shuffling strangers around all night.

He had the radio on but it was low. Not too low that we couldn't hear it, but not loud enough to force us to yell at each other if we wanted to make conversation. There was an array of water bottles stuck into the netting behind the front seats; hopefully, our Uber home has that too because I will not be having any water at this party. I guarantee my after-party kidneys will appreciate some water to end the night. The weirdest thing about this ride is how damn cold it is, it's like a fucking walk-in meat freezer in here, but Javi doesn't seem to be remotely affected by this chilling temperature.

Talia spoke up first, "Hey Javi, do you mind turning the AC off? Maybe bump the heat for a few miles, as much as I love popsicles, I don't want to be one myself."

Javi didn't respond.

Carter poked Javi's shoulder, "Dickhead, quit trying to freeze us and turn the heat on!"

Again, Javi didn't respond, and he didn't seem to care about the poke either. Carter and Talia moved close to each other for some body warmth. I decided I could use some of that, too, so I slid over to their side of the car. As I slid over, I noticed that Javi didn't have GPS on.

"Javi... how do you know where to go if you don't have the address entered into the GPS?" I asked hesitantly.

"Because I'm not taking you to your destination," Javi rebutted as he glared at me through the rearview mirror. "I'm taking you to my destination."

In that instant, we picked up speed... an uncomfortable amount of speed. The type of speed that keeps your back pressed hard against the backrest like those UFO rides at pop-up festivals. I couldn't move. Carter and Talia were also stuck pressed against the seat against their will.

The car took turns at lightning speed. We hit turns that didn't make sense, how could someone possibly have reactions this good? I don't think a professional driver could make the turns that Javi is consistently making.

After a few minutes, the car came to a familiar screeching halt. Thankfully, we all had our seatbelts on still, so when we were abruptly ripped out of warp speed, we just jolted forward quickly, then slammed back into the seat we were all just glued to. We were so shaken that no one noticed that the driver's door was open and Javi was gone.

"WHERE THE FUCK IS HE?! I'M GONNA RIP HIS FUCKING HEAD OFF!" Carter roared as he unbuckled and threw his door open into the darkness.

The door didn't recoil back into him, it was thrown so forcefully that it was now stuck open. Talia and I stayed in the car, we didn't want to see what was about to happen. I've seen enough of Carter's fights to know this won't end well for Javi unless he has a gun or a gang of pals hiding in the darkness. Talia was on her phone, but I doubt either of us had a signal in whatever building we were parked in.

"What's taking Carter so long? Shouldn't he be back by now?" asked Talia.

That very instant, the front windshield cracked and caved in. Then the noises moved to the side of the car that Carter exited. All along the passenger side window there was a dark streak accompanied by a crunching, yet wet, squeal. After it covered the stretch of the front window there was a loud thud followed by the broken door being slammed shut.

Talia scooted back toward me and shakily asked, "Carter? Please tell me that's you, I really want to go now. You taught him a lesson, and from the looks and sounds of it he won't be able to do this again even if he wanted to."

There was nothing, no response.

Then, the window of the door that was slammed shut started to shutter and creak. Slowly the window started to cave inward toward us, barely cracking under the pressure. I knew it was going to shatter at any second, so I shielded my eyes and turned away just to be safe. I was right, the window gave out and glass flew everywhere.

As soon as I felt the glass hit my feet, I unshielded my eyes and turned to face the window. Between me and the window was Talia, but she didn't take the same precautions as I did, she had glass shards sticking out of her throat and face.

Her throat was pulsing like she was trying to take a breath or say something, but there was too much glass in the way to even make a sound. She turned slowly to face me. I couldn't find any words to help her, so I sat there in silence as I watched her choke on glass and bleed to death. Our eyes met for a second. When they did, I noticed her eyes went wider than I ever thought human eyes could get.

I started to reach out my hands to pull her close, so I could comfort her in what would definitely be her final moments. My hands reached her shoulders and I drew her body close. I immediately felt the warm rush of blood, significantly more blood than what I saw on her before I pulled her in.

Freaked out, I pushed her back, thinking that moving her somehow made her condition worse. It wasn't me that made it worse. After I pushed her back to where she was, her body continued backward and then slipped onto the floor. But her head remained there, still staring at me from its original position with her big wide eyes.

Her left eye started to twitch, then it started to pulsate until it popped out of its socket and my gaze followed it as it rolled to the floor. I've never been so terrified in my entire life. It's the type of terrified where you're weirdly calm but could shit your pants at any second. I gained enough resolve to return my gaze to Talia's face, that was a fucking mistake. This whole night was a fucking mistake, what in the wild FUCK is that?!

From Talia's eye socket slithered a long tendril of some kind, accompanied by one from each of her ears, and one from her mouth, four of them in total. They appeared to be sniffing the air in my direction as they crawled through the air. The tendrils came roughly four inches from my face, did one more sniff, then in sync, they all opened up revealing a row of fangs dripping with blood and screeched into my face. But they didn't lunge, it was almost like they didn't have enough slack, what the fuck are they tied to?

The tendrils retracted, and as they did Talia's lifeless head fell to the seat and rolled toward me. I swatted it away, I missed the first few swats but eventually hit her right in the neck where she had been detached from her shoulders. I panicked and went to wipe away the blood I thought would be there, but my hands were dry, Talia's head had no blood to spare.

The door across from me began to open. No choice left, I opened my door and made a run for it. I have no fucking clue where I am, where I'm going, or what I'm even running from. But as soon as I made it a few feet from the car, my path was blocked.

It was Javi, he was standing a few feet from me but I could still make out his features even in this darkness. He raised his hands to his face and put them both in his mouth and gripped his lower jaw. Then he started to rip his own mouth open, the skin stretched to an inhuman length but it never ripped or cracked.

The sound of the skin being stretched to such a length sent a shock of unease through my body, but I couldn't stop staring. It was as mesmerizing as it was terrifying. Javi finally finished stretching his jaw, his chin was now resting roughly in the center of his chest. From the depths of his mouth slithered the four tendrils from earlier. Now I know what they were tied to, preventing them from devouring me the same way they did to Talia, and I assume Carter.

Before my life flashed before my eyes, I took a quick glance around me hoping to fuck that there would be a way out of this shit. Or at least something I could use as a weapon. When I glanced left, there was a large pile of bodies... wait, pile?! OF BODIES??!! AM I IN ITS FUCKING LAIR??

Of fucking course this is a lair for some fucking tendril bloodsucker. After that quick meltdown, I took a glance to the right. A few feet away, there was a large wooden splinter lying on the ground. It looked pointy and long enough to use as a spear. I'm confident I can throw it, I threw javelin in college, so surely I can throw that hunk of wood. It's only been two years.

So that's the play, it's decided. I jump for the splinter and toss it at Javi and pray it impales the piece of shit before his mouth tendrils relocate all of my blood. The tendrils opened up and screeched in sync all over again, but this time they lunged at me with murderous intent. I immediately threw myself toward the wood splinter as they snaked through the air. They hit the air where I used to be and screeched between one another and tried sniffing me out like they had before.

Their lack of eyes buys me just enough time to pick up the makeshift spear and gain decent footing so I can really put my back into this throw. I aim by pointing my free arm at Javi and imagine a straight shot at his chest. I pull the spear as far back as possible, plant my feet, rotate my hips harder than an NFL quarterback so I can add as much power as possible, and fling that spear like my life depended on it... because it did.

My aim was off, I didn't hit his chest, but I hit something better, his big fucking head. The spear went straight through his right ear and out his left ear. Javi started shaking violently, the tendrils flopped to the ground after a sad hiss. He pulsated for a few seconds, then one at a time his arms and legs snapped and bent inwards toward his chest until he was a floating ball of flesh with snapped bones jutting out in various places. The tendrils got sucked into the center of this flesh ball, it sank inward like it just exhaled its final breath, then it exploded.

Millions of pieces of Javi were sent flying, but before a single piece of him could reach a surface to stain, all the Javi pieces burst into ashes and got carried away into the darkness. I called the police, answered their questions, and went home. I deleted Uber from my phone.

I think I'll use Lyft going forward.

Jacob Anderer is an aspiring author who is working hard on his debut novel. Born and raised in Wisconsin, he is an avid gamer, is very big into anime, and enjoys anything horror-related. His love for horror began when he was very young and saw *Goosebumps* on TV.

He has always been intimidated by writing, but his wife and child give him the courage and support he needs to follow his dreams.

"Lydia and the Lesson of Lovers' Lane"

Lydia and the Lesson

of Lovers' Lane

By Shannon Frost Greenstein

T he woods were dark. His hand was creeping up her
thigh.

"Kyle?"

Swedish Death Metal poured from the dashboard
speaker, the steady heartbeat of a bass line resonating deep
within Lydia's back teeth. The road was rougher now,
practically nonexistent, deep ruts in the ground speaking to
the generations of young people who had made this drive
through the years. The car shuddered and wobbled over rocks
and hummocks – its ancient shocks no match for the
topography of a deciduous North American forest floor – and
Lydia braced herself against a passing wave of nausea.

"Kyle, seriously. Would you just focus on driving
already?"

It was a full moon. The mess of trees and underbrush
outside Lydia's open window was misty and ethereal with
light. It was the height of summer, it was preternaturally hot,

and Kyle's air conditioner didn't work. Lydia was already lifting sweaty locks of hair off the back of her neck in the futile hope of catching a breeze.

Kyle left his hand where it was. "I can't help it. You drive me crazy."

He flexed his foot harder against the accelerator as if to illustrate just how crazy she was currently driving him. The tires immediately bumbled over an errant branch lying along the narrow road – an inadvertent guard rail courtesy of Mother Nature – and Lydia was thrown roughly against her seat belt.

"Kyle, Jesus!"

Kyle braked with a jolt and whipped his hand back to the wheel. Lydia was unsurprised to realize she did not miss it on her thigh.

"Sorry, hottie."

The stars were bright this far from the lights of the city; the crickets were singing a discordant harmony. The track issuing from the speaker switched to something punk and angry, as Kyle's hand found its way back under Lydia's skirt.

She sighed inwardly and stared out the window. It was Saturday night, and they were driving to Lovers' Lane.

It had already been a long evening. There had been ninety minutes of an action movie she never would have chosen. There had been two hours of a meal, showcasing the most awkward attempts at conversation she had ever endured. There had been Kyle's pleading as they left the theater to accompany him on "a really quick drive to see the best view in town," something to which acquiescing seemed easier than arguing at the time.

"We're almost there. I still can't believe you've never been out here before."

Lydia was initially pleased when Kyle texted, proposing a date for the evening. From what she could recall from last weekend's party, he was deliciously handsome and a phenomenal kisser. There had been a gin bucket at the party, however, and the world was spinning pretty merrily by the time she and Kyle exchanged phone numbers at the end of the night; she admittedly did not remember much about any conversations they may have had.

However, now that she knew how boring of a human being Kyle was – now that she was currently god-knows-where in the heart of the woods, heading further and further from her Egyptian cotton sheets and her bedtime skincare routine – Lydia was beginning to have serious regrets about agreeing to this late-night excursion. Damning her habit of people-pleasing, damning her inability to say, "no", she decided it was finally time to manage expectations.

"I can't stay that long..." Lydia started to hedge. "I have a lot to do tomorrow."

"Oh, trust me, you're not going to want to leave. It's a really nice view."

Given Kyle's roaming fingers, Lydia was pretty certain the view had nothing to do with Kyle's ultimate vision for the evening. But – that being the case – she was also certain he was about to be seriously disappointed.

They were driving further up now, the incline steep and the engine straining. Lydia's ears popped as the country-pop track flooding from the dashboard assured her she'd never seen a truck like this here truck. Just when Lydia expected the transmission to blow or the suspension to snap or the entire contraption to shut down entirely, the ground leveled abruptly. Kyle swung a sharp left, and suddenly the woods were behind them, the road reassuringly smooth beneath the wheels once again.

"Thank god," Lydia muttered, unclenching teeth she was unaware she had been clenching.

Another thirty seconds, another sharp turn, then the city stretched out before them across the broad expanse of the forest through which they had just traversed.

"Well?" inquired Kyle proudly, throwing the car into park and gesturing out the windshield. "What did I tell you?"

"It's something," Lydia agreed, her suspicion that the destination would be anticlimactic instantly confirmed. "You can see everything."

But it was nighttime, and it was late, and all there was to see were lights. There were glowing columns of windows from the downtown high-rise stairwells and repeating patterns of stoplights along the residential corridor, and the occasional flash of LED headlights. There was a smattering of twinkles from the cornfields to the west and a handful of neon signs from the 24-hour fast food restaurants and the entire night sky of stars above their heads.

Lydia looked at the lights, then looked at Kyle. She glanced at her watch and did some arithmetic. Exhaling heavily, resigned to the encounter but intending to wrap things up as quickly as possible, she fished through her purse for a Tic Tac and waited for the inevitable.

"Did I tell you how good you look tonight?" Kyle began, unbuckling his seatbelt as he turned to face Lydia, reaching out a hand to caress the sweaty tresses hanging next to her face. "You make me so hot. I want..."

"Me, too," Lydia interrupted. Remembering Kyle's proclivity for kissing, eager for a silver lining to this entire lackluster encounter, she leaned into his gym-honed body and closed her eyes, pouting her lips expectantly and crunching through the remnants of the Tic Tac.

They canoodled for several minutes, Lydia gracefully relocating Kyle's hand each time it crept up under her skirt. She was enjoying the rush of oxytocin; she was enjoying his fingers in her hair and his mouth against her neck. She was finding the whole experience slightly tedious but not entirely unpleasant when Kyle's fingers abruptly left her leg and began to fish in the pocket of his cargo shorts. Lydia sensed the crinkling of the condom wrapper even before she heard it, so choreographed and predictable was this entire maneuver.

Not much going on under that hood, her brain commented, and Lydia was inclined to agree.

"What are you doing?" she questioned immediately, sitting bolt upright in the seat Kyle had just reclined to lay at a 180° angle.

"Don't worry," Kyle crooned, bending to press his lips against her throat once again.

Suddenly, an ear-splitting alert erupted simultaneously from both Lydia's and Kyle's phones. Lydia winced and fumbled blindly in her bag to locate the device, while Kyle cursed and grabbed his own phone from the dashboard.

"Is there, like, an Amber Alert or something?" Lydia inquired as her fingers searched through old tubes of lip gloss and a fortune in spare change. Just her luck if now was the moment the globe was starting to devolve into nuclear holocaust and she was missing the alert to Duck and Cover because of Kyle, for Christ's sake.

Kyle scrolled down on the screen, his eyes shifting as he read the message. "It's just the news," he answered disinterestedly, returning his phone to the console, turning back to Lydia, his hands once again reaching hungrily for the waistband of her skirt.

"What about the news?" Lydia pressed, finally locating her own device as she sat herself rigidly upright, resisting the gentle pressure Kyle was applying to lay her back down against the seat.

"Who cares?" Kyle voiced. "Are you sure I shouldn't get the condom?"

Lydia did not respond. She, too, was reading the news alert, far more invested in the text than Kyle appeared to be.

"Oh, shit," she muttered softly. Still staring at the screen, she turned to address Kyle, her eyes wide with surprise. "There's, like, a psycho-killer on the loose right near here. Listen to this."

Exhibiting an exquisite understanding of UX design in the digital age, the alert boiled down the prescient information into bullet points. In a show of conditioning that would have made Pavlov proud, Lydia clicked automatically on the proposed hyperlink. A browser opened on her phone and an article from the local news publication slid into view.

"There was this kid in Belfast who was accused of burning down his family home, but he was never convicted, so he came to the U.S. as a teenager. He went to jail in the 80s for sexual assault, and he was apparently, like, legit crazy by the time he got out. Then it says he went on a serial murder spree and the cops were chasing him all over for a whole bunch of years. He's been up in Byberry right in the city ever since, but he broke out this morning."

Lydia was paraphrasing, skipping over extraneous details like, "Irish Republican Army" and "Schizoaffective disorder", speaking more and more quickly, her voice vacillating with a dreadful kind of wonder. She rushed over descriptions of murder scenes and bloody evidence until she arrived at the crux of the story, pausing for effect and to ensure Kyle was still listening.

"They say he lost a hand during The Troubles. They say he has a hook instead. They say... he uses it to disembowel his victims." Lydia delivered these facts in a tone steeped with drama like she was reciting a Shakespearean soliloquy and Kyle was a packed audience at the Globe Theater. Finally, raising her eyes from her phone, Lydia was bewildered to find Kyle staring back at her blankly, like she hadn't just revealed there was a disemboweling Irish serial killer at large.

"Well?" she asked breathlessly.

"Wow," Kyle voiced obediently when it became clear a response was expected. "That's intense."

Lydia inhaled, preparing to fill in the specifics she had left out, preparing to describe the man's escape in exquisite detail. To compare the entire affair to Edmond Dantes' breakout from the Chateau d'If if Edmond had dug himself out with a hook.

It took only the briefest of moments for the words bubbling behind her tongue to die before they could be expressed, however, as Kyle's hand furtively slipped back into his pocket and emerged clutching the brightly wrapped condom once again.

"Are you kidding?" she inquired incredulously.

"What?" Kyle asked defensively. "What did I do?"

"Aren't you listening?" Lydia snapped.

"Yes! I heard you! A serial killer from Ireland. But, like, what's the big deal?"

"Because he's on the loose!" Lydia reminded him, frustration rendering her typical speaking voice a squealing soprano. "He's supposed to be right around here!"

"Look, babe, he's probably far away by now. And I'm sure they're gonna catch him any minute."

Kyle sounded irritated and impatient like Lydia was the one making things difficult, like Lydia was the issue with this entire situation and not the possibility of being gutted by a giant (and presumably dirty) hook on the end of the arm of a raving madman. She bristled, taking immediate umbrage with Kyle's tone, not to mention the condescension with which he was minimizing the admittedly slight – albeit very real, in her opinion – chance they could be in danger.

Apparently, sensing this glimmer of Lydia's darkening mood from her body language, Kyle abruptly changed tactics and dropped his voice to a low purr. "Just relax. You're so beautiful. I want to kiss you for hours."

"Would you tell me something?" Lydia inquired with feigned sweetness. "What is it about this situation, precisely, that you think I find sexy?"

Kyle stared back wordlessly, aware something was expected, uncertain of when he needed to have this response prepared. The condom hung limply from his fingers like a plot device by Chekhov, though Lydia knew of at least one ordnance that was not being fired tonight.

"Why, out of all the things in the world I could be feeling at this exact moment, is your first guess Lydia must want to get laid?" she questioned. "Is it because you think mortal peril turns me on?"

"Ok, fine, I get it," grumbled Kyle. He returned the condom to his pocket, his face bearing a look of sour exasperation and bitter disappointment.

"Or are you convinced the threat of a serial killer pales in comparison to the glory of your penis?" Lydia continued.

"I said ok already!" Kyle snapped, slamming his hands down on the steering wheel.

Lydia jumped at the sudden noise – even more on edge by the news alert than she first thought – and glared at the individual she once found really cute but now found nearly intolerable.

They sat in charged silence for a few seconds. Lydia was about to suggest they head back to town when Kyle spoke up once again.

"I mean, why did you agree to come up here if you didn't want to fool around?"

"Are you kidding?" Lydia sputtered back. "I'm here because you begged me to drive up with you to see the view. I didn't even want to come!"

"Well, obviously I thought you wanted to! You've been coming on to me all night!"

Lydia blinked. She didn't even know where to start with that one.

"It's just not cool to send signals like that if you don't want it," advised Kyle sagely, rich with life experience and the infinite wisdom that comes from being young and male. "No one likes a tease."

Lydia was suddenly seething, rage bubbling up from her toes like magma. "Excuse me?" she spat. "What on Earth have I done to make you think I want to have sex with you?"

"You seemed pretty willing at the party last week," Kyle accused. "And you came up here tonight."

At a loss for words amidst all her fury, Lydia just gaped. She tried twice to respond, failed, took a minute to draw a gasping breath, and tried again. "What... what makes you think... I never said... you were the one who wanted... you don't automatically get to have sex just because a girl agrees to go on a date!"

Kyle rolled his eyes, as if that statement was too ridiculous to warrant any actual consideration, then jammed the keys back in the ignition. "Whatever," he declared. "Let's just go."

"Let's," agreed Lydia shortly, turning her body to stare fixedly out the window.

Half an hour, max, and you'll be back between Egyptian cotton sheets, she assured herself. *Hang on, and this date will end.*

She didn't turn around as Kyle grumbled and refastened his seat belt; she didn't turn around as he twisted the key. It was only after a stretch of silence, the jingling of the keyring, more silence, some clicking, and the lack of an engine turning over that Lydia finally shifted around in her seat to glare at Kyle.

Kyle, however, was not glaring back. Kyle was fixated on the dashboard with a face of consternation, his lust forgotten and his annoyance dissipating away.

"Shit," he stated conversationally.

Lydia waited for any sort of follow-up, but nothing was forthcoming. Kyle continued to fumble with the keys, the car emitting another series of strange clicks and then falling silent once again. He pumped the gas pedal; he shook the keyring. Finally, he threw up his hands in disgust and pounded the steering wheel a second time.

"Dammit!" he barked – a cliché of a reaction if ever there had been a cliché before – and Lydia struggled to keep from rolling her eyes. Still fuming, she chose instead to stay quiet. There was no way she was going to be the first one to end this stand-off. She was not going to lose to Kyle in a battle of wills.

Outside, a cricket began to sing. A cloud drifted over the moon. It fell darker if that was even possible, and in the shadow of the woods, Lydia suddenly felt very insignificant and far from home.

"The car broke down," Kyle finally announced unnecessarily.

"Obviously," Lydia muttered *sotto voce.* Then, beginning the search through her purse for her phone, she turned back to Kyle and raised her voice.

"Who should we call?" she asked. "Do you have roadside assistance?"

Now in planning mode, determined to fix this debacle as quickly as humanly possible, Lydia was already Googling nearby mechanics when Kyle eventually spoke up.

"I'm just going to go get my buddy. He has a tow truck."

"Why don't you call for one?" she inquired.

He looked at her as if she was slow. "Because my buddy has a tow truck. It's free."

Lydia started to protest, stopped, started over, stopped, gave it some thought, and gave up. "Ok. Fine. Whatever."

She waited to hear what would happen next, assuming it would involve her rescue in some way, shape, or form. Kyle proceeded to unbuckle his seatbelt, then stuffed his phone into his shorts, turned expectantly toward Lydia, and pocketed the useless keys.

"You ready?" he quizzed, and Lydia literally laughed aloud.

"I'm not going to go traipsing through the woods in the middle of the night just to save $50 bucks when there is a psychopath on the loose," she snapped.

"Well, what do you want to do?" demanded Kyle. "Are you just gonna wait here?"

"No!" Lydia exclaimed. "Did you not hear the part about the psychopath?!"

"Well, call an Uber, then," he snapped.

"I'm not waiting here alone!" she retorted. "They make Lifetime movies about situations like this!"

"Jesus Christ," Kyle spoke in a quiet mumble, an attempt to remain inaudible at which he was nearly successful.

"What's that?" Lydia questioned sharply.

Kyle heaved a gigantic sigh – Atlas with the world on his shoulders – and threw himself back into the seat, displaying at least a rudimentary knowledge of the way society views those men who abandon their women in the face of danger.

"Fine. Fine. I'll wait," he griped. "Just... order it already."

Lydia reached for her phone, watching Kyle out of the corner of her eye to see if he was about to do anything else snarky. He stared resolutely ahead, however, so she pulled out the device and opened the Uber app.

Marveling at precisely how much worse this date had become, Lydia typed in her address. Her point of origin auto-filled with their current location, and she was grateful. She had no idea where they were, to be honest, and was feeling more than a little disoriented with the moon obscured and the forest looming spookily behind them.

"It says ten minutes," she proclaimed, her eyes already glued to the miniature sedan making infinitesimal progress across the two-dimensional map on the screen.

"Great," answered Kyle sarcastically, the back of his skull against the headrest, his eyes closed, simply oozing boredom and petulance.

They sat, as an owl hooted and a siren wailed in the distance and the minutes ticked by. They sat as the digital Uber inched along the digital road, as Lydia's deliverance approached the lookout point, as a disconcerting clunk rang apropos of nothing from under the hood of Kyle's useless vehicle. They sat as a second news alert lit up both their phones – *Escaped convict still at large, considered extremely dangerous!* – and Lydia did her best to stop visualizing a host of serial killers with bloody hooks for hands crouched just beyond her periphery.

It was an exceptionally long ten minutes.

Finally, finally, brilliant light illuminated the interior of the car as the Uber pulled up behind them, headlights shining merrily.

"It's here," Lydia ultimately announced, when it became clear Kyle was making no effort to get up, to escort her to the waiting car, to bid her farewell like a gentleman, to make some attempt at adhering to the social norms that dictate what to do at the conclusion of a date.

"Ok," responded Kyle.

He did not bother to open his eyes, and Lydia was struck by a wave of absolute disgust with dating, with men, with Lovers' Lane and hooking up, and Kyle's broken car. Where did she keep finding guys like this??

"Kyle, there's a murderer out there," she said evenly. "Can you at least, like, walk me to the Uber?"

Jaw clenched, Kyle exhaled deeply, and Lydia knew – she just knew – that he was silently commending himself for his chivalry, that he was already planning to disclose to his buddy how well he dealt with the hysterical chick who teased him all night and then refused to put out. He got out of the driver's seat, crossed in front of the car to stand directly in the headlights of the Uber – leaving Lydia to open her own door – and stood with his arms firmly crossed, deliberately refusing to meet her eyes.

"Bloody hell," Lydia declared under her breath. She dropped her phone in her bag, heaved the straps onto her shoulder, exited, and slammed the door with a bit more force than necessary. The night was muggy and still; Lydia thought again about the disemboweling Irish hook man and broke into gooseflesh nonetheless.

The Uber was a nondescript SUV colored in a nondescript earth tone – function over form – with bubblegum pop drifting through the open windows. It sat idling not far from where Kyle's sedan had shuddered its last breath, and Lydia was grateful for this proximity. She could not help but feel cowed by the density of the woods and the enormity of the trees above her, an eerie scene even without the threat of an errant sociopath with sinister intentions drawing ever closer.

She stalked past Kyle, the SUV's lights illuminating him from behind like a Renaissance halo, and headed for her four-door salvation.

"Thanks, for everything," Lydia declared sarcastically, not bothering to wait for a response.

Kyle garbled something inarticulate and fell into step beside her. He gestured impatiently at the backseat as they neared the Uber, so Lydia delighted in taking an additional moment to compare the SUV's license plate to the image in her app.

They matched, of course – who else would be up here this late unless expressly summoned? – and Lydia climbed into the car with a sigh of relief.

"Bye," Kyle offered brusquely. He shut the door behind Lydia and stomped away toward the woods without looking back, ostensibly beginning the trek to save $50 on a tow.

"Hi, sweetheart."

The Uber driver was an older woman with cat-eyed classes and hair dyed a ghastly shade of red. She exuded comfort that was downright grandmotherly; it stood in direct juxtaposition to the past three hours of anxiety with Kyle, and Lydia relaxed for the first time since the sun set.

Reminding herself yet again that she deserved so much better, she smiled at the driver and pulled out her phone, already mentally composing the message to her roommate to describe this utterly disastrous evening.

"Where are we going, love?" asked the woman.

"Back to town, right off Main Street," Lydia confirmed, her fingernails clicking as she shot off a string of exclamation points in a text.

"Ok, we'll have you home in just a few," the driver chirped, fussing with the GPS, adjusting the speaker volume, positioning the rearview mirror. Then she paused, squinted, turned to the backseat.

"Was that you?"

Lydia engrossed in telling her BFF about the part where Kyle pulled out the condom, looked up inquisitively. "What?"

"Never mind. I thought I heard something. Probably a branch on the roof."

Lydia craned her eyes through the window at the woods and the world beyond. There was no motion; there was no noise. The humid air hung heavy over the night, not even a breeze to rustle the leaves. The woman shrugged, shifted, and met Lydia's eyes in the rearview mirror.

"Let's blow this joint, girlfriend, you look like you've had a night."

Lydia laughed as the driver dramatically peeled away, and felt the scrim of the terrible date begin to lift from her skin.

The drive back down through the woods seemed to go much faster than it did on the way up, probably because she wasn't fending off advances from Kyle. Preternaturally chatty, the driver kept up a string of commentary as Lydia recounted the past several hours.

"Sweetheart, take my advice," she advised at the conclusion of Lydia's saga, as they emerged from the woods and merged onto the highway. "Get a cat and a vibrator and forget all about little boys until you're paying your own way. Then you can maybe find a real man, just in case you ever want a distraction."

The driver spoke as someone who knew, and Lydia felt a rush of kinship, a sense of solidarity with a complete stranger, connected as they were in their joint belief about the uselessness of the 21st-century male specimen.

They were both belting The Divinyls' *I Touch Myself* by the time the SUV pulled over to the curb in front of Lydia's apartment building. Minutes away from her nighttime moisturizer and down pillow, Lydia had never before been so grateful to see her apartment.

"Thanks so much," she gushed to the woman behind the wheel, who acknowledged the gratitude with a cheery wave.

"You have a good night," the driver instructed her. "I'll wait until you're in the door."

Silently thanking the God in whom she did not believe that her Uber driver was a woman who understood the hazards of womanhood, Lydia tossed her phone in her purse, gathered the straps over her shoulder, and opened the back door.

"Thanks again," she spoke into the interior of the car, then slammed the door closed.

It took only a few steps, with the help of the hazy light from a blinking streetlamp, to notice all the blood on her hand.

Feeling sticky, examining her palm, gawking with befuddlement at the dark stains highlighting the whorls of her fingerprints. Lydia did not make the connection for several seconds. When she finally did, she found herself frozen in place, jaw agape, unable to form her next coherent thought.

Turn around and look, she commanded her body.

Not a chance, responded her brain.

Dimly, in the midst of this silent mental battle, she heard a lilting voice call out, "You ok, honey?"

Unable to respond, the question nonetheless broke Lydia's spell, and – very much against her will – she slowly spun back to the vehicle.

Hanging from the door handle by its razor-edged point was a sharpened metal hook, the steel gleaming even under the night sky, the bright blood splashed along its length completely unmistakable as anything else.

"Honey?"

Staring dumbly at the blood on the roof, at the maroon streaks dripping down the door, Lydia's brain was still refusing to cooperate with her limbs.

"Are you ok?" The woman was calling through the open window, looking unsettled, looking apprehensive.

Lydia ignored her, still unable to speak, and focused instead on locating her phone in the depths of her bag. After a few seconds of futile searching, she upended the purse right on the sidewalk, receipts, pennies, and rogue makeup brushes spilling onto the concrete with a clatter. With shaking hands, she picked up the phone, pulled up her call list, then pressed a number. It rang and she began to pace. It rang and she wrung her hands. It rang and she met the gaze of the Uber driver, her eyes hollow and haunted. It rang, and rang, and rang.

But Kyle never did pick up.

Shannon Frost Greenstein (She/Her) resides in Philadelphia with her children and soulmate. She is the author of "The Wendigo of Wall Street," a novella forthcoming with Emerge Literary Journal. Shannon is a former Ph.D. candidate in Continental Philosophy and a multi-time Pushcart Prize nominee.

Her work has appeared in McSweeney's Internet Tendency, Pithead Chapel, WAS Quarterly, Bending Genres, and elsewhere. Shannon was recently a finalist for the 2023 Ohio State University Press Journal Non/Fiction Prize.

Follow her on her website at shannonfrostgreenstein.com or on X and Bluesky at @ShannonFrostGre. Insta: @zarathustra_speaks

"Living Picture"

Living Picture

By Michael Paige

F ucking perfect, I thought as the storm released sheets of rain over the canopy. Lightning lit up the sky in a brilliant stitch of fire followed by a powerful bellow. I was leaning against one of the tapered columns with my shoulder bag. My ride, who swore to me he'd be back after the show, still hadn't returned from his drink run. No phone call. No message. He was probably passed out at home drunk as a sailor, a very stupid sailor. As undependable as he was (and as much as I wanted to ring his neck right now), I couldn't help but thank him for setting this gig up for me in the first place.

If not for the last-minute recommendation, Godfrey would have found another Disc Jockey for his house party. It wasn't a huge gig, but any extra penny helps. But where did that leave me now? Stranded in a rainstorm with a house filled with grad students too high or drunk to find their own feet, let alone hold a coherent conversation. No soul here was fit to give me a lift, and like hell, I'd stay the night in this place.

I cautiously peeked at the time on my phone: 1:25 AM. Together now: *fucking perfect*.

"Sorry about that, little lady," Godfrey said, floundering out of the doorway. He was wearing a dark plum Willy Wonka-esque coat. "I got your pay right here. Thanks for the show. You really got a knack for this, huh, Sam, wasn't it?"

"You got it, thanks for booking me," I said, collecting the money and also catching a sweetly bitter whiff of the burnt herbal scent drifting off of him.

"Pleasure." He grinned at me and then whistled at the flooded walkway. "Man, it's really coming down tonight. Are you still waiting for your ride?"

"Yeah, hopefully, they'll be here soon."

"Let me know if you could use a ride. Hell, you could even stay here if you wanted."

Tempting as the offer was, the suggestive look that carried it made the offer almost laughable. The sort of way a butcher ogles a slab of meat.

"No thanks, I'm good." I buckled my lips into a dismissive smile.

"Suit yourself, then," he said and sauntered back inside where the warmth was.

I returned to rain-watching. Anybody I could call would be asleep by now. Well, almost everyone. No—I shook the thought immediately. Even if my father did decide to help, his teeth would sink into me so deep he'd taste the marrow. "What were you thinking? No backup plan? No plan B? Why do I always have to save you from yourself, Sam?" Sure, that's just what I needed to do, hand him the perfect I-told-you-so scenario so he could massage that irritating father bravado.

After Mom fell into a coma, he sort of did too in his own way, only waking up to be a father when it was convenient for him. Bitter thoughts encrusted with raw irritation brushed against my skull at the mere idea.

"No thanks, not going to happen," I whispered to the precipitation ghosts. Come to think of it, this house wasn't too far from the station on 23rd Street half a block or so. The subway would save me the expenses of calling for an Uber. No doubt it was more of a pain in the ass. But a pain in the ass meant less money out of my pocket. What was a little wetness anyway?

My equipment packed in the gig bag, I slipped a bud into my ear, unfurled my umbrella, and walked through the swelling puddles. The rain pelted my face with a cold mist. I was tired. And fat lady Misery was beginning to hum a few bars. But I still had the music in my ear, and that was all I needed to get by. It wasn't the money that solely drove me here; it was mostly the passion.

Once that first track starts, my heart disappears. Regrets, money troubles, memories... nothing else matters but the music. There isn't any other feeling in the world like the rush of energy followed by a crowd's euphoric screams as they flail their arms like mental patients. My mind feels like a blowpipe shaping molten glass bubbles into something different, something new. Sometimes I even forget to breathe; it's too easy to lose myself in the harmonic flow vibrating my organs.

It didn't take long for me to reach the gleaming wet intersection of Fifth Avenue and Broadway. I crossed the relatively quiet street to reach the northbound entrance to the terminal. Two lamp posts were casting a brilliant glare with green tops and milky white bottoms. A homeless man was curled over a thin sheet of cardboard at the foot of the stairs, taking shelter from the storm. I maneuvered my heavy bag to the shoulder farthest from him. If the man tried anything, he'd get a lovely taste full of the mace stowed in my pocket.

Lucky for him, he only shifted sleeping positions as I passed by and continued down the mezzanine. I bought a ticket from one of the machines, slipped it into the turnstile gate, and found more stairs. They led me to the boarding area next to the track. The air was permeated with that familiar damp, guttery, metallic funk. When I was nine, I called them train farts. There was a woman here, too. She was aimlessly walking between the columns, cradling a baby in her arms as she did so. It was sort of an odd look, given the time and place. She was wearing an ivory-white puffer jacket with a fur-trimmed hood.

Soon enough, a quiet gliding hum sounded from the tunnel. Out came the piercing spotlights followed by the high-pitched electronic whine that reverberated off the walls as the N train rolled to a stop. The platform screen doors slid open and were joined by a pre-recorded (strangely melodic) voice.

"Stand clear of the closing doors, please!" There was a note of challenge in the warning, as though the voice were daring you to do the opposite.

I wandered inside and sat down in one of the powdery blue bucket seats. The woman followed after and took a seat a few rows in front of me. Her skin was a yellowish color, suggestive of severe jaundice. I leaned back and blew a warm burst of air over my fingers. It was a home stretch now, the worst part of tonight was behind me.

"Stand clear of the closing doors, please!" The robotic voice chimed again as the doors simultaneously slipped shut. The gliding hum returned, and the underground train pulled forward with a jerk.

Within seconds, the music in my ear was replaced by a painful crackling hiss. I pulled out the earbud and popped in the second one. It worked fine for a minute before succumbing to the same static screech.

"Come on, come on..." I moaned, so much for the anesthetic. Some rain probably slipped through my hair and ruined them. From my peripheral, I noticed the woman suddenly stand up from her chair and wander down the aisle.

She was walking with a suspicious slowness. When she was parallel to me, she reseated herself. My eyes instinctively dropped to my phone to avoid an uncomfortable staring contest with a stranger. I then looked up and realized the woman wasn't taking her eyes off me. From this close, I could see the unhealthy pastiness of her skin and the gauntness of her features.

Her black hair was short, only reaching her sullen cheeks. Her eyes were green and looked to be struggling to stay open. There was no whiteness to them, only red nets of popped blood vessels surrounding abnormally long pupils. It looked like Coloboma, or, Cat Eye Syndrome, an eye condition I read about on the internet once. When she noticed I was now returning the look, her tight lips puckered into a humorless smile.

"I'm sorry, can I help you with something?" I asked.

The woman's hourglass-shaped pupils perked at my question. "I'm glad you're here, really, the poor thing wasn't going to last much longer." Her voice was dull with fatigue. "Not going to last long at all."

Just as I stood up to find a different seat, the woman leaned forward and whispered to the infant in her lap. A few incoherent muffles slipped out. The strange woman then sat up straight and brushed away the covering from her child's face. But it wasn't a child I saw, far fucking from it. Its uneven skull resembled a skinless grape with clusters of forked veins branching throughout its thin skin. Its mouth (if it was a mouth) was a lipless vestigial slit. The circumference of its translucent head was taken up by two eyeless sockets draped on the inside with lines of stringy tissue.

I was left standing there stunned, attempting to fathom exactly what I was looking at. At that moment, bands of its straggly eye material tightened like a balled-up fist in both of its sockets. A terrible pulsating pain suddenly condensed in the center of my head. My ears started to ring. The throbbing tightness in my skull increased to the point where I collapsed back into the seat. It felt as though someone was hammering an invisible stake into my brain like into a vampire's heart. I couldn't move. My arms and legs felt like mud. I couldn't scream. *Stand up, just stand up*, I begged my uncooperative muscles.

The warped mass of a head remained motionless, save for its eyeholes full of clenching meat threads. More of the strands twitched and convulsed into tight knots, working in tandem with the pain, the vivid paralyzing pain. The lights were unsteadily flickering.

I was forced to watch as transparent flaps unfurled from both sides of the thing's head. They folded into equiangular spiral shapes. Another clump of skin in the center of its face protruded outwards. The clump molded into some sort of limpid nose. That was when I realized those folds on its head were ears. Not only that, was the thing *bigger* now?

Yes, it was. The woman confirmed this as she lifted the entity from her lap and gently placed it on the seat next to her. It was the size of a small toddler now. Its boneless-looking limbs hung like shriveled chicken legs. Thin worm-like threads wriggled out of its broad scalp that soon became wet clots of black hair. Its limbs started to thrash about as though they were being shocked by short electric bursts. I could hear the muffled sounds of joints grinding together and popping out of place repeatedly. They were stretching, growing longer. Even its skin was changing into a healthy fleshier color like a chameleon manipulating its own skin cells.

The invisible stake pushed further into the cluster of nerves behind my eyes. I thought I was bleeding, but it was only hot tears rolling down my cheeks. I'd have given anything in the world for the pain to stop. Little by little, change by change, the being was beginning to take on the physical semblance of a young girl. A few forked black veins still lingered beneath its fake-pigmented skin. There was a vertical scar below its belly button, the same scar that I had.

But that made no sense. My scar was from an ovarian cyst surgery when I was twelve, why would it have the same scar? Then I saw the birthmark on its right shoulder, my birthmark. I realized that it wasn't an invisible stake being plunged into my skull, it was a straw.

This thing—whatever in God's name it is—was sucking up my memories, sampling the different flavors, and enjoying them. What is going to happen? I wondered, what is going to happen when there are two of me?

"I know it hurts," the woman said with a perceptive nod. That disembodied stare on her face made my stomach churn. "I'm sorry for this, really, I am. But such things are necessary for us; they are necessary for our survival, you see?"

The humanoid thing was now a naked living picture of me, except for the straggly jungles in its sockets. It stood upon its bare trembling legs and took an indecisive step toward me. I wanted to scream, but all that came out was a raspy whimpering.

An abrupt female recording then sounded over the intercom. "Next station, 14th Street."

That was it, the next station! If just one soul were waiting on that platform, they'd see me. They'd see the woman with the fucked up eyes. And they'd see the naked humanoid standing in front of me. The naked unpolished version of myself continued toward me. Two fingers on its left hand split open. Slender filament-like stalks bloomed out of them and squirmed as though tasting the air.

The dark windows soon became lit canvases of the platform. One person, just one, I begged the cosmos. But a glance through the window told me nobody was there. Every second that passed was another chunk chipping off my freedom. The doppelganger bent over and extended its hand with the dancing filaments toward my face. *Eyes!* I screamed internally, *it wants my eyes!* It counterfeited everything else, but why not the eyes? Maybe the woman's pupils were the result of them trying.

The high-pitched whistling came, the N train suddenly stopped abruptly. The stop-in motion jerked the doppelganger off balance yet again. For a moment, only a moment, the pressurized stabbing pain dissipated. It had lost its unseen grip on my mind as the subway doors slipped open. Without hesitation, I rooted my fingers into my back pocket. The eyeless version of me returned its gaze. Just as the kaleidoscope of pain started to bud, the mace canister was already in my hand. A fine aerosol spray of burning chemicals drenched the thing's face.

That caused it to let out a horrific, unearthly shriek.

The woman from her seat started to scream as well, spitting out random gibberish as though her tongue were stuck to the roof of her mouth. She suddenly jetted from her seat and rushed me. I emptied another burst into her exposed face which made her writhe away in shrieking fits.

Fat membranes of yellow froth emptied out of the doppelganger's stringy sockets and oozed down its cheeks. A horrible smell of ethanol, insect repellent, and raw sewage struck my nostrils. That horrible piercing shrill was like a broken siren. I gripped the body of my shoulder bag and lifted it over my head. Without even thinking, I smashed it over the thing's skull.

Expensive equipment rattled inside. Still, the ululating persisted, louder than ever. I rushed past the subway doors and ran like hell up the stairs. The screams of the woman and the thing wearing my face reverberated off the walls. Even as I reached the street again, I could still hear them.

The rain hadn't let up. I ran until my legs forced me under a shop's canopy. This was no doubt 14th Street, but my mind was racing too fast to recognize anything. Unconsciously my fingers were already curled around my phone and dialing. My dad picked up. I told him everything in a panicked mess. He told me to stay where I was; he was coming to get me.

Who was going to believe me after this? Probably nobody. Not the police, not my family, not my friends... no one. Maybe Godfrey had slipped something into my drink before I left, maybe I had caught the second hand of something during the show. What I witnessed on that subway felt so unreal, it had to have been in my imagination. Surely, they'd have cameras down there, right? I sucked in a deep breath and tried to control my throbbing chest beneath the awning, waiting for someone to come and find me.

No matter how hard I try, I will never be able to rip that image out of my mind, crawling around my nightmares, twisting into something so pure and deceptively innocent.

A woman with a baby in her arms.

Michael Paige's work has been included in several literary magazines such as The Furious Gazelle, The Scarlet Leaf Review, MetaStellar, Midnight Magazine, The Horror Zine, as well as printed & digital anthologies for Savage Realms Press, Crimson Pinnacle Press, Ill-Advised Records, Gravelight Press, October Nights Press, Media Macabre, Little Red Bird Publishing, Chilling Tales for Dark Nights, Culture Cult, Skywatcher Press, Wolfsinger Publication, Jayhenge Publishing, Wicked Shadow Press, Moonday Mag, Eerie River Publishing, Dragon Soul Press, a charity anthology for Great Lakes Horror Anthology (GLAHW), and most recently, The Final Passenger Anthology.

"End of the Line"

End of the Line

By Leigh Kenny

T he passengers lurched forward in their seats as the bus
rattled to a stop on the darkened street. Evelyn peered
over the headrest before her and watched as a young
woman stepped from the pooling shadows and boarded.

The woman stood at the front of the vehicle, her eyes
darting nervously around her like a rabbit caught in a beam.
Her face was vaguely familiar. As the bus resumed its journey
with a rumbling shudder, she swayed on her feet and wrapped
the long, wool coat tighter around her slight frame.

Beneath the coat, the end of a brightly-coloured
patchwork scarf poked out. Evelyn watched impassively as the
girl continued to scan the seats, her scuffed, trainer-clad feet
taking the first tentative steps along the aisle.

Apart from Evelyn, and now the girl, the bus held only
men. Behind the driver, two elderly gentlemen sat, their heads
almost touching as they conversed in hushed tones. A couple of
seats back, and across the aisle, a middle-aged man in a rumpled

suit sat with a battered briefcase clutched to his chest. Like the girl, his eyes darted around nervously, as though he expected someone to materialise before him and snatch his precious cargo away.

Evelyn didn't blame him. She had heard that muggings and assaults were a frequent occurrence on public transport in the city, and the odds increased ten-fold at night. Behind the businessman, and just a few seats ahead of Evelyn, sat a small group of teenage boys. They whispered and giggled amongst themselves as the bus lumbered along the quiet city streets.

Evelyn sat alone in the middle of the vehicle, and behind her, raucous whoops and hollers filled the space between. The back seat and the few seats orbiting it were home to a small group of young men. The clink of bottles was just audible enough for the other passengers to know there was a party happening, one they weren't invited to and one they'd best not interrupt.

As the girl moved slowly along the aisle, she caught the attention of the back-seat dwellers, who began whistling and barking salacious comments in her direction. Evelyn could see the panic cloud the young woman's eyes as she looked at the other passengers helplessly. Before the woman could catch her eye again, Evelyn turned her head to look out the window, her own reflection a ghostly apparition that haunted the space between her and the rain-slicked street outside.

"Mind if I sit?"

Evelyn turned to answer, but before she could, the woman dropped wearily into the seat next to her. Behind them, disappointed groans and laughter floated on the stale air, the clink of bottles resuming in earnest.

"I don't mean to invade your space, but if I sit anywhere alone, the guys at the back will make it their mission to harass me. I'm on the night bus more than I'd like to be, so I know the drill," the woman said, turning to Evelyn and extending her hand. "I'm Casey."

Smiling weakly, Evelyn shook hands with the girl. She looked to be in her late twenties, though her elfin face and freckled nose lent an innocence to her features. The hair that peeked from beneath her rain-splattered hood was mousy brown, and she had an altogether plain and non-descript look about her.

Except for her eyes.

Her blue eyes were large and expressive. A spark of intelligence emanated from them, and the longer Evelyn looked, the more the feeling of recognition grew.

"Do I know you from somewhere?" she asked.

"Depends. If you're a regular in the city morgue, then perhaps."

Evelyn hissed a sharp intake of breath, and the girl, Casey, threw her head back and laughed, a deep and throaty chuckle.

"That always gets people," she said with an impish grin. "I'm a tech in the morgue. It's not nearly as exciting as you'd think, and the hours are shit. That's how I've come to be a regular on the night bus. I had a car, but I hate driving in the city, and parking can be a nightmare, so public transport seemed the better option." She flicked her head around, taking in the gloomy bus and its passengers before turning back to Evelyn, one eyebrow arched. "Kinda rethinking my life choices, though!"

Despite herself, Evelyn chuckled. She was warming very quickly to the personable young woman beside her. And with the journey that lay ahead of her, a distraction couldn't hurt.

"I'm Evelyn," she said, smiling at the girl. "I'm not from around, just staying in the city. I'm meeting someone, that's my reason for being here. In hindsight, the night bus might not have been the wisest option."

"We gals got to stick together, Evelyn," Casey said with a wink, as she readjusted her scarf. "I'll make sure you end up where you should unless my stop comes up first."

"I'd imagine you'll be gone before I reach my destination," Evelyn replied. "My stop happens to be the end of the line."

"Same! Who are you meeting? Tell me to mind my own business if I'm being too nosey."

Evelyn glanced down, fidgeting nervously with her fingernails. "I'm heading to see a young woman I knew in another life," she said quietly. "Velma Kelleher."

Casey slapped her arm gently, her eyes wide. "No way! I know Velma! She lives a street over from me. I took her under my wing when she first arrived, and we became friends. I told you, us gals got to stick together."

Evelyn smiled at the enthusiastic woman beside her, but her lips wavered, and the smile strained to reach her eyes. She still hadn't quite gotten over the shock of hearing from Velma in the first place. "Oh. Do you know her well?" she asked.

"As well as any friend, I guess. My shifts are crazy, so I've never had time for 'close, personal friends' but we've had coffee a bunch of times, and she knows where to reach me if she ever needs anything," replied Casey with a shrug. "Are you family?"

Eyes wide, Evelyn stared at the other woman, but before she could reply, Casey continued, "She always seems really delicate. Velma did tell me once that she always expects her family to come looking for her someday. She seemed pretty scared! She told me that her mom tried to kill her! Can you believe that??"

Evelyn whipped her head around, her eyes widening in shock.

Casey nodded. "That's what she told me. Said that her mom was a single parent for the first few years of her life but then she met a guy, a police officer. They had a couple of kids together. Velma said the guy, her new dad, never really liked her, but once her brothers came along, things got way worse. She said he tortured her. Psychologically at first, but it escalated to physical violence pretty quickly. She didn't say it in so many words, but I gathered that things took a pretty sinister turn. I think he might have done something else to her..." Casey looked at Evelyn, her eyes conveying the words she didn't want to say out loud.

Reading between the lines, Evelyn gasped again, her hand fluttering to her mouth.

Casey nodded gravely. "Yea. That. So anyway, Velma says she went to her mom, and she didn't believe her, accused her of being jealous and trying to cause problems within the family. She said that from then on, her mom changed, and things got even worse. I was shocked. And then she goes and tells me that her mom and stepdad tried to kill her. Drugged her and tried to slit her throat, but I guess they messed up somehow. They left her in the woods. An old mountain man found her and looked after her until she was well, then she struck out on her own. She was only ten years old! Can you believe that?"

"Velma always did have quite the imagination," Evelyn chuckled. "I knew her as a child. Know her whole family. They're good people. Why didn't she go to the police if things were so bad?"

"I asked that," said Casey, matter-of-factly. "She said that because the guy, Dean, I think was his name, was a police officer, she was afraid to go to any authorities. I think she was scared that they wouldn't believe her, or that they'd close ranks to protect one of their own. But I dunno, it all sounds very fantastical to me. And she never mentioned it again, except that one time not long after I first met her."

Evelyn smirked. "Yep, that sounds like Velma. Fantastical."

Casey glanced sideways at her, the passing streetlights outside casting shadows over her face. Only those bright eyes were visible in the roiling gloom. "So, you are family?" she asked.

Lifting her head, Evelyn scanned the bus, only noticing now how empty it had become. One by one, the other passengers had disembarked, spilling out into the gloomy streets as each destination was reached. So engrossed had she been in conversing with the girl beside her, that she hadn't noticed that they were the last ones left aboard the bus.

"I'm more of an old friend," she said, turning back to Casey with a tight smile.

Casey grinned, then carried on talking, her shoulders and hands in constant motion as she talked about some recent unusual cases at the morgue where she worked, the state of crime rates in the city, and the cost of groceries with inflation.

Evelyn continued to smile and nod, occasionally interjecting with a short response. All the while, she silently wished that the girl would stop talking or move to another seat in the now empty bus. She needed time to ruminate on the meeting she was soon to have.

The road whipped by, the hazy glow of the streetlights becoming more and more occasional as the bus drew further away from the populated centre of the city. The buildings grew smaller, their facades more tired. Dark alleyways littered the sidewalks between buildings, their gaping black maws suggesting all kinds of hidden horrors. As the streetlights grew scarcer, so too did the people, and Evelyn felt a growing pit of unease spread throughout her old bones like a cancer.

She gazed out the window, the apparition of her reflection in the glass joined by that of the animated girl beside her. Slowly, as the bus trundled on, the streets began to show signs of life once more. Neon signs heralding bars and clubs whipped by the window, small groups in their immediate orbit, and stragglers branching out into neighbouring streets. The tight fist of unease in her stomach began to loosen. For someone who preferred her own company, Evelyn sure felt better being surrounded by people.

The bus sailed along, the urban district slowly becoming more residential. Streets branched off the main thoroughfare on which they travelled. Some wider and more populated than others. Large townhouses mingled with monstrous apartment blocks, small mini markets, and all-night diners lighting up the spaces in between.

The bus slowed to a crawl before chugging to a shuddering stop by a shadowed bus shelter, its perspex surround cracked and mottled with age and neglect.

"Last stop, end of the line." The bus driver stood and looked pointedly down the aisle at his remaining two passengers, before stepping off the vehicle.

Following Casey out of the seat, Evelyn peered through the windows, watching as the grizzled old man sparked a flame and lit the cigarette that dangled from between his whiskered lips.

"You're heading to Velma's place?" Casey slowed her pace to match Evelyn's, her breath puffing out before her in tiny clouds that rose into the sky before fading to nothing in the cold night air. "Her street is the one after mine."

Evelyn nodded, grateful once more for the company. The prospect of navigating these unfamiliar streets alone in the dark chilled her.

"This way," Casey called cheerfully, veering onto the cracked sidewalk and disappearing among the shadows. Quickening her step, Evelyn marched after her into the darkness.

Casey continued to chatter as they walked, and Evelyn was glad that the younger woman was so unaware of her discomfort. She was also glad that the young woman seemed to prefer talking about herself. Casey didn't seem to realise that she was oversharing with strangers, strangers who did not share in return.

Slowing her pace, Casey turned to Evelyn at the mouth of a narrow laneway. "This is me," she said with an apologetic smile. "Next street over is Velma's. Just look for the Hope Street sign, it's bolted to the wall. Great to meet you, Evelyn. Tell Velma I said, 'Hey!'." With a wave, Casey turned and strolled down the laneway, the coloured tail of her scarf flipping behind her. The absolute darkness swallowed her whole until all that was left was the echo of her footsteps.

Evelyn stood for a moment, listening as her companion's footsteps faded away and she was alone again, only her tumultuous thoughts for company. She walked quickly along the pavement, her heavy coat pulled tight around her. As she approached an opening ahead, she lifted her eyes. Sure enough, barely visible within the dull glow of a lone streetlamp, was a grubby metal sign.

Hope Street.

Turning the corner, she was greeted with a street, not much wider than the one that had swallowed Casey just minutes before. Evelyn took a deep breath to steady her quavering nerves, then headed down the street, her ears straining to hear anything that might be waiting in the darkness. Small alleys branched off the main street like skeletal fingers, each one cloaked in shadow.

"Number Ten. Number Ten," Evelyn whispered to herself as she walked along the quiet street, her eyes scanning the building numbers as she passed each one. Finally, Number Ten appeared, the brass numerals fixed to the wall.

The townhouse loomed over her, silent and dark.

"Looks abandoned," she muttered to herself, as she climbed the stone steps and reached for the doorbell.

Nothing happened when she pressed the bell, and with a grimace, Evelyn raised a fist to rap on the door. As her hand connected with the wood, the door swung inwards, its aging hinges creaking loudly under the pressure. Stepping into the darkened hallway, Evelyn called out, her own voice startling her in the silence.

"Hello? Velma?" she called, hating the tremor she heard in her tone.

The hallway stretched from the doorway, disappearing somewhere deeper in the house. A light clicked on suddenly in one of the adjoining rooms, a triangle of light slicing through the gloomy hallway.

"In here," called a familiar voice.

Evelyn could feel her pulse surge. Even after all these years, she still knew that voice, it seemed. A mother's love was truly enduring. Her forgiveness, not so much.

With steely determination, she strode down the hallway and toward the inviting strip of light. Stepping through the doorway, she was greeted by a punch of cold air somewhere in her gut.

"Ooooff," she moaned, dropping her hands to her burning midsection. Her fingers met cold steel, and tears formed in Evelyn's eyes as her daughter stepped closer, her fist wrapped around the hilt.

"Hello, Mom," said Casey. She pulled the blade from Evelyn.

The sucking sound of steel leaving flesh seemed to reverberate around the room that was empty but for a wooden chair and a table. Evelyn stumbled, and Casey caught her roughly by one arm, then guided her to the chair. Through fluttering eyelids, Evelyn took stock of her surroundings.

The walls of the room were covered with peeling wallpaper, the pattern long since faded. Stuck haphazardly around the room were photos of her daughter. Two-year-old Velma, grinning at the camera. Four-year-old Velma, staring in wonder at a tiny ladybug that perched on her chubby finger. Five-year-old Velma, a shadow of a smile where a grin had once been. Seven-year-old Velma in the background of a picture of her two younger brothers, her eyes puffy and red, and ringed with circles as dark as bruises. Nine-year-old Velma curled into a ball at one end of the sofa, her stepdad and brothers on the opposite end, her stepdad's fingers outstretched as he tried to pull her onto his lap, a place she did not want to be.

So many pictures, each a snapshot of a little girl's life ruined by those she trusted to protect her, until finally there were no more pictures. No more life. Evelyn cried softly, her body slumping in the chair. Casey stepped forward and pulled the phone from Evelyn's pocket. She checked that there was no passcode, then double-checked that the information she wanted was there. Dropping to her knees before the older woman, she slowly unwound the patchwork scarf from around her neck and let it fall to the ground. Evelyn gasped at the ring of delicate scar tissue that decorated her throat like a necklace.

All at once, the pieces fell into place. That familiar feeling she had when Casey first stepped onto the bus. The questions about Velma. The oddness of Velma reaching out to her at all after all this time. And after all that had happened to her. All that Evelyn had allowed to happen.

"Velma?" she whispered, her voice choking.

"Velma doesn't exist anymore, Mom. And neither do you." In a flash, Casey pulled the knife across her mother's throat with a flourish, the steel biting into her flesh like butter.

Evelyn gasped and raised her hands to her throat, but nothing could close the gaping wound inflicted upon her. As blood, so crimson it was almost black, flowed down her chest and saturated her clothes, Evelyn choked and wheezed. Her body fell heavily to the floor, and as her eyes began to glaze over, she watched as her daughter emptied cans of gasoline around the room.

Shaking the last of the fluid onto her mother's trembling body, Casey moved away, flicked a lighter, and tossed it at her. As the flames engulfed the room and burned the flesh from her muscles, Evelyn tried to scream.

Nothing but a gargled whimper escaped her as she succumbed to the darkness. Casey walked from the room, the childhood pictures that had kept the fire burning inside her for so long blackening and turning to ash, as she passed them like a phoenix rising from the flames.

Casey knew she had sacrificed Velma's life, just as her mother had done all those years ago. It was necessary, though. The only way she could see justice done for the little girl she had once been. The phone in her hand vibrated then, the screen lighting up. And in its sickly green glow, a name.

The name.

Dean.

Tucking the phone in her pocket, she skipped down the steps. Heading toward the closest alley, the one that had taken her to this street less than an hour ago, Casey quickened her step. The next bus out of town was due soon; she had places to go and people to visit. The night sky behind her began to light up, shades of orange and red bleeding into the blackness, as the flames devoured the house on Hope Street and all it contained.

Casey didn't turn to look. She slipped into the mouth of the alley where the shadows waited, and the darkness stole her away.

Leigh was born and raised in the garden county of Wicklow, Ireland. She lives by the Irish Sea with the love of her life, two wonderful boys, a black Labrador, and a three-legged cat that hates people.

You can find out more about Leigh's work and any upcoming releases on her Facebook and Instagram pages: LeighKennyWrites

Her debut novella, Cursed, is available here: https://mybook.to/Cursed-LeighKenny

"Atlantean Migration"

Atlantean Migration

By Barend Nieuwstraten III

Agnes pinched her nose and gently attempted to exhale through her clamped nostrils, redirecting pressure to her ears to counteract and prevent them from popping. It always made her think of her Uncle Alistair who, due to some operation or accident, was able to make smoke come out of his right ear when he'd take a puff of his pipe and pinch his nose shut.

As a little girl, it had always made her laugh.

Sitting aboard the Pontus, she was thrilled to be a part of such a rare and unique expedition. The maiden voyage of a new deep-sea engine. A submersible vehicle beyond the mere sink-and-hoist diving bells or short-range craft that skimmed the floor of rivers, harbours, and bays. The Pontus was a feat in nautical engineering and a marvel of the dawn of the twentieth century. Ferried out across the Atlantic by ship, it would dive deeper than any vessel had ever done, in the hopes of locating the lost continent.

"Don't often see a lady in coveralls," the man in the next seat commented.

They were one of four pairs of passengers in the cabin.

"Would it be unladylike to admit that they're surprisingly comfortable?" Agnes said, brushing at her murky yellow jumpsuit with brown leather segments. "It feels a little like the pyjamas my mother put me in when I was four. I feel a tad juvenile in them." Agnes smiled. "Doctor Agnes Pelton-Grace," she said, holding out a hand to shake.

"Professor Allen Dennington," he replied, taking her hand. "Doctor, aye? What's your field?"

"The study of marine life, primarily flora."

"A marine biologist? Impressive. Though, how exactly would that really pertain to this expedition?"

"Technically a marine botanist. My particular field of interest is coral. Mister Ellington is confident I should be able to shed additional light on the research depending on how various colonies may have developed over any ancient structures, or if indeed they are concealing any. What about you?"

"Well, it seems your field may be growing all over mine. I study ancient architecture, focusing primarily on the Greek variety. Hopefully, the observatory down in the... basement. I don't know nautical nomenclature, but Ellington's boasted quite a collection of advanced telescopic and periscopic lenses."

"They'd need to be," Agnes said, patting her hand on the wood paneling beneath the porthole. "We're never going deep enough to see anything out these windows. The pressure would squash us like an egg."

"Raw or boiled?" Allen said, fingering his collar nervously.

"Would it make any difference?"

He thought about his query a moment and chuckled at himself. "I suppose not. Aside from a crushed boiled egg being easier to clean up than a raw one."

"Best not to think about it."

He slowly nodded, looking past her to the window beside her. "It's already getting dark out there. We're not that far into the descent already, are we?"

Agnes followed his gaze and leaned in toward the thick layers of glass. She looked up and saw a school of fish swim away from their large vessel that was probably the size of a blue whale. At least one with a large pot belly, in which the observation deck was located, in what her fellow passenger had called the basement. She glanced at the others with whom they shared the seating area. All too busy looking out their nearest portholes, also sitting in pairs and quietly talking amongst themselves. Strapped securely into their seats for the initial dive, they had only the opportunity to meet those seated next to them. She looked at her safety harness, only to be released by members of the crew upon reaching a specific depth.

As time passed, it grew colder within the cabin. Steam was channeled through large black pipes above them, serving as heating elements. Agnes's right hand shook as she waited for the temperature to rise again. She felt the pressure building within the vessel as if some tropical snake was wrapped around her head and slowly tightening. She rubbed her temples and stretched her jaw to stifle the discomfort. There were creaking sounds in the wood and tinging in the metal hull.

"What's that?" she asked.

"I think in its own way, the submersible is feeling what we are," Allen said, raising his palm and curling his fingers in as if he was closing his grip on something. "Don't worry, it just means the ocean's trying to crush us like an egg, but our shell's too tough."

Though still rubbing her temple, Agnes smiled at Allen's throwback to her earlier deep-pressure remark.

"And yet, I feel a little scrambled."

"Well, if it doesn't pass, I believe one of the officers is a doctor, from memory."

Agnes nodded and turned toward the window as a flicker of light and shadow caught her periphery. Something outside the porthole.

"What is it?" Allen asked.

"I'm not sure. A bit of light, but I swore..." Agnes said, moving her head about to see what she thought she saw.

"Swore what?"

"Something rushed away from the hull."

"Well, it looks like they lit the port and starboard lights. They must have startled some poor sea creature away."

She pressed as close to the glass as she could to look down and saw particles in the water like floating dust illuminated by light coming from the side of the vessel. "Oh, yes."

She nodded, recalling smaller glass domes placed about the Pontus from the outside. She had assumed them more portholes when she was boarding. "Yes, little gaslights and reflectors, just so we have something to look at. Of course, they have an array of them at the front of the vehicle. From what

I've been told, the belly of the craft has the really impressive ones. Designed to help us see deep down below."

The cabin temperature slowly grew comfortable, but Agnes's right hand was still shaking. She felt an odd unease, something beyond the foreboding of being deeply submerged in the middle of the ocean. It wasn't just that the next gasp of air outside the vehicle was too far above to hope to reach in a single breath, certainly making the lifejackets under their seats only useful for the first minute of their initial dive. She felt like an intruder in someone else's domain. None of them belonged down here. It was one thing to take to the skies in zeppelins, but there was air up there.

This was a buried coffin. They were out of their element and in someone else's. She wondered if that someone had just fled the outer hull of the vessel as the lights came on. As she looked out for the mysterious figure, Allen was looking out past her but far more excitedly, merely eager to see what wonders of the deep he might observe. He was like a child at the zoo. She found it calming, along with seeing the other three pairs seated in the cabin, all leaning toward their nearby portholes.

Voices of the crew echoed from elsewhere within the Pontus as valves and pistons changed their rhythm of hissing and clicking. Soon a uniformed officer attended the passenger cabin. It was not a naval uniform but that of the private organisation that commissioned Ellington's expedition. If not his own.

Agnes wasn't entirely sure of the arrangement.

"Greetings, esteemed guests," the young officer said. "For those of you who may have forgotten, I'm Mister

Belle-Vue. The Pontus is moving to within observable range of our destination and in a moment, as we cease our descent to maintain a consistent depth, you'll be free to roam the vessel. Though, Mister Ellington will be expecting you on the observation deck, so perhaps roam down there first." He offered a charming smile and most of the group chuckled in their safety restraints.

After refreshments were served, a crewman and a medical officer checked each of the passengers, one by one, before unfastening their harnesses. The medic had each passenger say their name and count to ten, while checking their pulse, and examining their eyes, asking them how they felt. When he finally got to Agnes, she offered her left wrist, loath to expose the tremor in her right. She feared being left strapped in her chair if she exhibited any weakness.

"How do you feel?" the doctor asked, after getting past the initial questions.

She dug her fingers into her thigh with her right hand. It helped control the shaking and helped her focus on speaking clearer. She slurred a little counting to ten, which she put down to nervousness. "Like the air is hugging a little to tight," she said. "But otherwise, I feel fine."

"That's the pressure," the medical officer said, with a reassuring smile. "You'll probably get used to it."

He gave the crewman a nod and her restraints were unlocked and unfastened. She followed the others through the front of the cabin onto a small set of descending stairs that took them through lower decks and into a room with minimal lighting where Mister Belle-Vue and Mister Ellington were waiting.

There were two island workbenches built into the ship with glass tops from which a blue glow emanated.

"Ah, Doctor Pelton-Grace," Ellington said, running his hand over his slicked-back brown hair that highlighted his receding widow's peak. He gestured for her to join him at one of the benches. "Just in time. Look. The coral valley below is awaiting your professional gaze."

Agnes leaned over the bench and looked down. She found herself peering through a series of great square lenses like a telescope in which the raised bench was perhaps the top third of the full structure. It was hard to gauge the length through the cumulative magnification of the multiple layers that blurred in the corners, making what she saw feel as though she was seeing through the eye of a fish. Or at least how she imagined it would look to do so. Columns of light shone down into the water from a series of illuminative devices arranged around the viewer. In the centre, she could see the ocean floor or at least a large shelf. As he had described, there was a landscape of coral below.

"Astounding," she said. "So many colonies fighting each other for dominance in a war that's raged for who knows how long."

"And over terrain you're the first to see," Ellington added before looking to the others.

"But what's under the coral? We have experts on topography, ancient architecture, geology... won't you join us and pool together your wealth of acquired knowledge to better inform us all of what precisely we're looking at?"

The others rushed to gather around the viewing stations, gasping and humming as they marvelled at the new depths being made visible to them.

"Yes," Ellington said, proudly. "Behold the new wonders of the deep. We are the fingertips of the hand of man reaching further than he ever has before."

There was soft chatter between those who'd come down from the passenger cabin, as they all leaned over the viewing benches.

"So?" Ellington eventually queried, warmly. "Initial impressions?"

"The coral valley seems to follow a natural trench," Agnes said. "Nothing so far to suggest a base of terrain made by human hands."

Ellington looked to one of the others who nodded in agreement. He gave a sigh of resignation but seemed far from defeated. "Well, it is still early, I suppose."

Agnes leaned in and squinted as she saw something swimming through the trench. "Do you see that?" she asked Allen.

"What?" he asked, trying to follow her eyes.

As she pointed, it slipped deeper into the trench and out of view. "I've lost it," she sighed. "It was long, like a shark but slenderer. Its tail seemed split or seemed, almost as if..."

"As if what?"

"As if a pair of legs," she hesitantly observed.

Allen gave her an inquisitive look, concealing an incredulous one.

"I'm not saying what I believe is down there, I'm describing what I saw from here, in a brief glimpse."

"What did you see?" Another guest of Ellington's asked. He was a lanky man with a narrow face.

"Some sort of..."

"Marine life," Allen finished for her. "A shark of some variety it seemed. Went into the crevice of the valley and slipped away." He imitated a swimming thing with his palm through the air, even though he'd entirely missed it.

"Oh, pity." The lanky man shook his head and looked back up to the pair. "Doctor Phillip Dent, marine biologist."

"Ah," Allen said with realisation. "The thing I mistook you for," he said to Agnes.

"I'll have to keep a sharper eye on the terrain ahead," Dent said.

Agnes smiled but felt suddenly light-headed.

***

Agnes awoke, staring at a bolted ceiling. She was lying down and blinked profusely to settle the unstable focus of her vision. She began to push herself up but felt hands gently grab her arms.

"Easy, now," the medical officer said, lowering back down from her left side.

Looking around she saw all the hallmarks of an infirmary, surrounded by medical equipment and an eye chart on the wall. "How did I end up here?"

"You passed out. Fainted. One moment you were talking about sharks and coral, then you were swaying and were fortunately caught by those near you before you fell. You might have hit your head on something and done real harm."

"I don't remember that at all."

"No? Well, fainting's a little odd like that. Sometimes you go all at once, sometimes bit by bit. But it's done now, so no need to fret. People often panic when they wake up from it. But you've been quite brave about it, all things considered."

"But why did I faint at all? The pressure?"

The medical officer nodded. "I should have been a little more thorough with my initial assessment before letting you out of your seat. You seemed quite resilient, and I took your word for it that you were simply nervous. More fool me," he said, raising his eyebrows.

"I felt fine at the time. I guess it just snuck up on me." She let her right hand slide over the edge of the bed to conceal the tremor she felt returning. "I feel fine now." She looked around the room, attempting to gauge the passage of time. "How long was I... incapacitated?"

"A little under an hour."

She bulged her eyes and pushed herself up. "Good lord, I'm missing everything."

"Well, I need to clear you before you can return to duty."

"Go on, then," she said, turning to face him as she sat up on the bed. She put both hands behind her back like a schoolgirl at assembly. She dug the fingernails of her left hand into her right hand. The pain helped her focus. "My name is Doctor Agnes Pelton-Grace. Marine botanist and coral enthusiast. One, two, three, four, five, six, seven, eight, nine, ten," she rattled off without slurring or stuttering. She smiled proudly, knowing that she had passed his feeble test.

He didn't seem a qualified doctor by trade. More a medical student, and an early one at that, poached from his study through whatever connection brought him to serve here. He was making far too much of her turn, and she wasn't about to miss the opportunity of a lifetime because of an overcautious, ill-experienced medical officer.

"Honestly, I feel fine. I must have just had a little too much wine with dinner last night, and it made me a little vulnerable to the pressure. But now I've had an hour-long nap and I feel quite refreshed."

The medical officer's eyes explored her face as if looking for an excuse to keep her detained but, in the end, he slowly nodded. "Very well. If you say so. But at the first sign of trouble, you come and see me. If you feel anything wrong, see something that doesn't make sense, have trouble putting words together, feel a loss of balance, then you have someone walk you back here, yes?"

Agnes disguised a grimace from her self-inflicted pain as a smile and nodded. "Of course."

Passing a porthole on her way back to the observation deck in the belly of the Pontus, Agnes noticed something strange about the passing reflection in her periphery. She took a few steps back as the image sank in. She saw a vague reflection in the glass, doubled by the surfaces on either side of the thick glazing. It was barely present with the low lighting within the vessel compared to the lights outside the ship illuminating the water around them.

She wasn't sure what she saw that first time out of the corner of her eye, but it was far bolder and more prominent than what she saw facing it directly. After a few moments, she dismissed it and continued on her way.

When she approached another porthole, she made a point of looking outside and slowed her pace as she began to pass it. The face she saw was not her own. Halloed by her own shallow reflections, the face she saw was barely human. Large black eyes looked back at her, sloping upwards toward the temples, and blinking, not with pairs of eyelids but a single strip of membrane that occasionally moved from side to side so that its vision was never completely impaired. Its skin was smooth and slick, pearlescent green, shining yellow and blue in the light. The corners of its mouth were webbed while gills opened and closed on either side of its neck. A masculine figure, even with its decorative fins sprouting from its jaw and temples. It looked mesmerised at Agnes, as curious to see her as she him.

There was a mound that vaguely resembled a human nose. Without nostrils, it seemed a vestigial homage to what must have once been human. Adapted to aquatic life over thousands of years, he was a miraculous achievement in evolution.

"Atlantean," she said, quietly. She examined his face as reason began to assert itself. "But how? How can you be? How could one adapt instead of drown?"

He pressed his hand against the glass, exposing his webbed fingers. After she stared at it for a while, she realised he was nudging his head toward it, gesturing to his own hand. Instinctively she pressed her hand against her side of the glass to correspond to his.

"Questions," a warm and gentle voice filled her mind.

It took her a moment to get past the intrusion and welcome the bridge across insurmountable states of existence. "Many," she said. "So many."

"The answers lay deep," the gentle voice in her head said. "Come to us and learn of all that we have become. Dive deeper."

"We can dive no further," she said. "We would not survive."

"Our ancestors feared the sea when it swallowed our home long ago, but then the becoming took place. Your ship may not survive, but if you came, you too would become."

"Become?" she queried with concern. "You mean change? Become like you?"

The aquatic figure before her gave a single nod. "This place is special. Our ancestors made it so. But you must come closer. You will learn nothing while so far away from our home."

Agnes looked to the direction in which she had been heading, toward the observation deck. She could hear the faint echo of all gathered down there.

"Everyone is there," the voice said. "Take the ship deeper and let them hear our voices."

Agnes nodded and made for the bridge.

At every porthole the Atlantean was there, swimming to the front of the vessel. Accompanying her on what she realised was a solo mission.

The others would not understand.

It wasn't the pressure affecting her, it was this mental connection. The Atlantean reaching out to its long-lost cousins of land. His voice had found her. More receptive than the rest, she had been chosen to facilitate the reunion between modern man and those of millennia passed.

The bridge was located at the nose of the vessel, boasting the most viewable vista of the ocean from within the craft. Beams of light reached into the dark deep blue ahead but there was nothing to be captured by the illumination in the endless depths that stretched to the Americas.

She looked through the round window in the door. Inside, a single officer had been left to monitor the controls. She raised her hand to knock on the door and saw the red cuts her fingernails had made in it to remedy the tremors. She made to gently test the door, but it was locked from the other side. There was no keyhole, which meant some sort of manual lock was on the door.

The door suddenly opened while she was studying it, startling her.

"Can I help you, miss?" the officer asked.

"D-D-Doctor," she corrected, straightening up. "I... ah... appear to b-be lost." She could hear her own words slurring and stuttering. She did her best to concentrate on sharpening them. "Can you direct me to the observation deck?"

"Oh, certainly, Doctor," the young officer said, keeping a foot in the doorway as he stepped partially out. "If you take the port passageway, you'll find access to the stairs on your left."

Agnes feigned confusion, pointing to the starboard passageway from which she had arrived.

"No, no, around that way," he stepped out a little further to point again.

"Sorry, the medical officer said I'm not responding all that well to the pressure down here. Perhaps it would be best if you just show me."

He looked back and forth, loath to leave his station. He took a few steps out into the corridor. "It's just down here, and around the first corner."

Agnes slipped quickly and subtly back into the bridge room and shut the door, finding a wheel on the inside of the door. Heavier than she anticipated, she turned it as quickly as she could. By the time he darted back to the door, the bar had been sufficiently fed through to prevent the door from being opened from the outside. The long handle jiggled, reacting to its counterpart on the other side, but the door was not going to budge.

He yelled and banged on the door with his fists, but he was greatly muffled. She stepped away from the door and looked at the controls. Too few were labelled or clear in purpose to allow her to take any great control.

Fortunately, the one component she was after was clearly labelled 'descent' and 'ascent' at either end of a handle that could only be pushed forward or pulled back.

She pressed forward hard.

The vessel continued forward for a moment before the nose could be felt diving, tilting the balance of gravity. Tiny particles in the water, caught in the light like fine snow, went from moving past the viewing window to seemingly moving upwards. The Pontus groaned as its iron frame and plating protested the stress of increased pressure, loudly banging, ticking, and creaking. A bell was ringing somewhere outside the bridge room. She had heard it when they made their first dive after separating from the ship that towed them out to the middle of the ocean.

The officer was joined by more uniformed men and crewmen. They were yelling at each other, then back at her through the thick glass. She heard a series of rapid cracks and turned back to see the outer layer of glass at the nose of the vessel had long white fissures in it. She heard panicked cries faintly through the door she'd sealed behind her.

For a moment, she was concerned that she had made a mistake, but the Atlantean pulled himself across the nose of the vessel and into view of the forward window. He offered a calming smile as he clung to the glass in all his evolutionary glory. His webbed feet were long like flippers and webbing extended between his upper arms and flanks. Shamelessly, without the robes or togas of his ancient civilisation, his people had clearly moved beyond such constraints.

She looked back to the door where the Pontus crew and officers continued to shout at her to open the door.

Agnes pointed to her aquatic friend. "Fear not the depths," she called out. "They have promised us adaptation. We shall see the lost continent for ourselves, with our own eyes, and become like him."

The panicked faces looking back were all struck with confusion.

"Doctor Pelton-Grace," the voice of Ellington spoke from within the room. "Agnes, wasn't it?" It was coming from a brass mouthpiece at the end of a tube, hooked to the wall. "Doctor, are you there? Can you hear me?"

She looked to the door, but there was no sign of him. He was calling to her from some other part of the vessel.

138

"Pick up the blower," he said, as the vessel continued to crank and bang about her. "Do you hear me?"

She did as he instructed and brought it to her mouth. "Mister Ellington?" she queried and brought the piece to her ear.

"Listen to me," he pleaded. "You must stop the descent. Portals are cracking. The ship cannot take these depths. We must return to a higher depth, or we will all be killed. Do you understand?"

"We shan't be killed," she assured him. "The Atlanteans will preserve us. They will alter us. They have that power. He has promised."

"What?" Ellington demanded.

"She's gone completely mad, sir," said another voice in whichever room Ellington was communicating from.

"Listen to me, Agnes, please. There are no Atlanteans. Only ruins somewhere below."

"No, a thriving civilisation who've crossed the barrier between worlds of air and sea awaits us. They have invited us."

"Agnes, the Atlanteans are long since drowned. Let us observe their world from a safe depth."

"You don't understand, Mister Ellington. We shall soon live amongst them. Be as them. Come to the bridge and see." She released the tube and walked to the forward viewing glass as the mouthpiece scraped across the floor, calling her name. The cracks in the outer layer were growing longer, and ocean water was spraying onto the next layer of glass, slowly filling the narrow space between.

She placed her hand on the glass nearest the Atlantean.

"Soon, we shall be together," his voice said, reassuringly inside her head. "They will understand once the becoming has taken place for them."

"Agnes!" Ellington yelled, now outside the door.

When she looked, water was spraying the men on the other side. Ellington was looking at her as she pointed to the Atlantean, but he scowled in fear and confusion.

"He will guide us," she said.

"Who?" Ellington yelled as those around him began to abandon the attempt to breach the door and moved as if wading in water.

Agnes furrowed her brow as she looked at her Atlantean friend. "Almost there," he said in her head. "Almost there."

There were screams outside the door. When she looked back, water was washing and foaming against the door's window. The sound of cracking drew her attention back to the glass before her. The second layer began to crack as water filled between the first two layers. The third would not be far behind. The air grew dense, and she felt as if her head was in a vice. She pinched her nose and blew through it to un-pop her ears. The room exploded into glass and water, almost instantly filling the bridge with freezing brine.

***

When Agnes reopened her eyes, she was hovering over a city of blue and green glowing lights. The Atlantean was holding her hands as they passed through warm currents. Holding her hands, they turned and twisted together in the water as if dancing some waltz.

Agnes smiled, calmed by the voice in her head, promising her all that lay ahead in the world below, at the bottom of the Atlantic Ocean. When she blinked, she swore she saw the inside of the Pontus's bridge, once more.

Filling rapidly with water that dragged her gasping and gagging for breath into the upper back corner. Fear and panic consumed her body as she floated to the last pocket of air in the broken vessel. Her nostrils and throat burned with brine as she cried out in regret and terror.

She closed her eyes tightly.

Now she found herself again in the Atlantean's embrace above his lost city, dancing the merman's waltz over his impossible civilization. Her new home awaited, and the sounds of a perishing vessel being consumed by the ocean faded, leaving behind the deep aquatic rumble of a place deeper than any man had ever visited.

She smiled in bliss as the lights of the underwater city dimmed slowly into darkness.

Barend Nieuwstraten III grew up and lives in Sydney, Australia, where he was born to Dutch and Indian immigrants. He has worked in film, short film, television, music, and online comics. He is now primarily working on a collection of stories set within a high fantasy world, a science fiction alternate future, often dipping his toes in horror in the process. With over eighty stories published in anthologies, he continues to work on short stories, stand-alone novels, and an epic series. A discovery writer not knowing what will happen when he begins typing, he endeavours to drag his readers on the same unknown journey through the fog of his subconscious.

Facebook: https://www.facebook.com/Barend3Author

Twitter: https://twitter.com/Barend3Author

GR: https://www.goodreads.com/barendnieuwstraten3

"Final Ride"

Final Ride

By Shawnna Deresch

M om told me the same story over and over again but added a new detail each time she told it. "We almost didn't make it to the hospital that day. You were close to being born in the back of your dad's old beater." She paused, then added, "Just like how you were made."

I cringed at the thought of my parents having sex in the back of the old wagon. Red dust from the coke ovens at the mills skirted the car. Dad opened the hood of the car and banged his head on it. Curse words streamed out of his mouth. It's the extent of his vocabulary. Drunk or sober. His fingers cracked with small fissures embedded with dirt and his yellow, nicotine-stained fingers revealed a man who lived a hard life even at his young age.

We sit in silence as the rusty station wagon rumbles down my street dipping into potholes the size of small craters, jostling me on the bench seat. A chain-linked fence surrounds corroded metal chairs sitting next to a concrete statue of

Mother Mary missing an arm in the front yard of the house I grew up in. They are swallowed into the other homes of my neighborhood, resembling a Mondrian painting in the sideview mirror.

I distract my mind by staring out the window, but the chaos floods my thoughts. Beads of perspiration dribble down the side of my face. I struggle to take my coat off as the heat in the car blasts in my face. I need to roll the window down. But the window won't budge, leaving me trapped like cargo in a box van traveling down the road.

"Can you put the heat down?" I ask the shrouded figure next to me.

It ignores my plea and continues to drive down the crumbly road. We pull into a parking lot at St. Martin Elementary School down the street from where I grew up. The four-story brick school building attaches to St. Martin's Cathedral. An imposing wood crucifix of Jesus guards the front entrance. A reminder of God's sacrifice of his only son so that I could be saved. I never needed that kind of saving. I think back to the last time I was in a church. Maybe when I made my first communion so many years ago?

My mom spat on her fingers and patted down the stray hairs on the top of my head. With her hands, she straightened the wrinkles out of my dress without success. Mother sighed disappointingly at me and walked to a pew. A white robe flowed to the floor with a crown of flowers that sat on my head. I shifted my feet from side to side too antsy to stand still.

How long was this going to take?

The crown of flowers dug into my scalp, and I scratched like a miner digging for gold. Behind me, Sister

Monica slapped the back of my head to get me to stop fidgeting.

"Humble yourself, child. Fold your hands in prayer like the other communicants." The parishioners none the wiser to her viciousness. Maybe she would remove me from the line of other seven-year-olds and make me stand in a corner like she did so many times before. At least I'd be safe from her wrath.

We are the only car in the parents' parking lot. I cross and uncross my ankles, restless and wanting to finish the uncomfortable journey. A grey cloud loomed near the sun and cast muted shadows on the playground.

A group of girls in plaid dresses with Peter Pan collars and puffy sleeves played hopscotch while one of the girls stood on the sideline with her stained, hand-me-down dress wringing her hands together.

She wanted to be invited to play.

I watched as one of the older girls walked up to her and snickered, "You can't play with us. Your dress is dirty, and your hair looks like a rat's nest. How did you get that scar on your forehead?"

The other girls laughed at the younger girl while pee streamed down her leg and puddled on the ground in front of her. Embarrassed, she looked down at her scuffed-up patent shoes.

I want desperately to jump out of the car and rush over to the girl sitting in a puddle of her own urine and tears to give her a hug, but the hooded figure drives out of the parking lot, leaving the girl in a fetal position to agonize over her own wounds. I press my fingers on my forehead outlining my zigzag scar.

Down the street from the school, we stop at the traffic light at the corner of Beech and Grove Streets. One Stop & Shop Liquor Store, the hub of the town, is open 24/7 and is a straight shot for the workers on their way home from the third shift at the mill. And where underaged teenagers solicit the homeless, whose tents are pitched on the sidewalk in front of the store, to buy them beer. Persuading them with food and money.

The light turns green, and the figure guns the car at the corner onto Grove Street.

"You took that corner a little rough there, didn't you?" I stare at the hooded creature hoping to strike up a conversation, but it continues to ignore me. I readjust myself on the bench seat in the old station wagon. The same car and corner my dad drove to Stop & Shop Liquor Store one night during a snowstorm. Snow collected in the cracks of the windshield. A kaleidoscope of shapes mutated every second as new snow slapped across the windshield faster than the wipers could keep up with.

I sat next to him, fussing with my doll's hair. He told Mom that he was going out for something, and he would be back soon. Her voice, a faint whisper, told him it was snowing outside. His eyes bore into her like a lion ready to pounce on its prey. She knows where he is going but doesn't say another word.

The snow fell heavier and covered the windshield the further we drove down the street to the store. Empty bottles of Jim Beam banged together at my feet. In one hand, he gulped down a bottle of bourbon whiskey while steering with the other, swerving to avoid the minefield of snow drifts. He overcorrected the wheel and we careened into a parked car. He sat slumped over the steering wheel with a bottle of Jim Beam still in one of his hands. My head banged against the dashboard. I reached to my forehead and sticky blood oozed out of a long gash onto my fingers.

"Please, turn the heat down." This time I beg the hooded figure. Instead, it growls a command at me, pointing its bony fingers toward a concrete building with a warped wooden sign hanging in front. A few of the letters fell off at some time, but the shadows of the former letters still linger as it read, *A Helping Hands Clinic.*

A young woman stood anxiously near the parking lot. Her belly barely showed a bulge, as she hid her stomach with her hands so the crowd of protestors wouldn't see it. With her head down, she scurried up the sidewalk to the front entrance, no one next to her side to support her decision. A man blocked her with his body. He towered over her and shoved a huge handmade sign in her face.

Choose adoption, not abortion.

A woman spit in her face. Like a ball in a pinball machine, she was bounced in all directions. The crowd encircled her like vultures going in for the kill. Vultures who chanted, "baby killer." The young woman stuffed her fingers into her ears to drown out the cries.

I want to scream, *it's my body, my choice,* but my voice is so faint that it's almost inaudible. A nurse from the clinic rushed out to help her. She screamed at the crowd to move out of the way and shuffled the young woman into the clinic. The figure steers the car away from the medical center. I bring my knees to my chest and hug them tightly trying to comfort myself, but grief overcomes me.

I barely notice we enter the North Regional Mental Health Campus toward a windowless building in the middle of the facility. A young woman with her arms wrapped in bandages hanging to her sides stood motionless.

"You are lucky to be alive," a huge orderly towered over her said.

Am I?

Crimson stains blossomed through the white bandages as the woman stared vacantly in front of her drowning out the whispers of the nurse and orderly huddled with the police officer.

"Please, let's leave," I beseech the driver.

We drive to the outskirts of town. The dome of the Johnson County Courthouse and Jail peeps over the silos and farms that dot the landscape. The figure drives to the courthouse's parking lot.

A young woman stood in a short-sleeved red jumpsuit strapped with a bullet-proof vest on the stairs of the courthouse with county sheriffs in full riot gear positioned between her and the combative crowd. Reporters posted up with microphones to capture any cries from the crowd or the woman. Hunched over, she sobbed uncontrollably. Her deceased boyfriend's family watched in the parking lot as protestors held up their signs in the air in judgment of the woman who sobbed before them.

"Murderer!" roared the crowd in unison.

Why did you persecute me? I was the victim of his abuse.

We continue our journey down the two-lane gravel road. For a moment, the sweet scent of spring lilacs tickles my nose. A moment with a thousand memories. Of some, I remember clearly, and others muddled by the burden of wounds people inflicted on me. A solitary tear trickles down my cheek and spills onto my t-shirt.

Oil drums erupting with fire line the road as we pass. Pungent odors like rotting meat crawl out of the barrels and seeps into the car. Bile rises from my stomach. Gravel scrapes across the undercarriage of the car as we come to a black metal gate flanked by a mangy, three-headed Cerberus guarding the entrance. Barbed wire fencing extends into the vastness on both sides. The gate slides to the side and we enter. It turns its head to me. For the first time, I see its skeletal face with two black holes where its eyes should be, maggots crawling out onto the rim of its hood.

"We're here," it snarls.

The figure's baritone voice echoes through me with an unnerving chill like ice sliding down my back which quickly melts as the heat in the car ramps up. The maggots crawl down its shroud and queue up in a procession toward me. I swipe them away from my arms and legs, but there are too many. I grapple at the door handle, but it's not there.

"Let me out!" I cry at the hooded figure, hoping he would release me. But my voice expels a medley of growls and snarls. "I want out!" I cry louder.

A chorus of unseen souls outside hiss and bark mocking me. The door swings open and I hurriedly exit the car wanting to run, but not sure where to go. The gravel crunches under my feet like crushed seashells on a beach. I squat down to pick up one. But it's not seashells, it's pieces of bone. Caring neither about it being human nor otherwise, I throw it back onto the ground and wipe my hands on the front of my jeans. Something hairy scurries across my feet and under the car to the other side.

The driver's side door creaks open and the figure steps out. A huge legion of lost souls wail in unison so loud that I have to put my fingers in my ears to stop the vibration of their cries inside my head. Scads of little hairy minions gnaw at my ankles, nipping at my skin, leaving blisters and open wounds as they work their way up my body. In the distance, illuminated by the fiery oil barrels, deformed creatures crawl toward me, their mangled appendages reaching out for me. I glance to the side to find an escape route, but the creatures are too fast. They grab and spit at me. One tears my flesh apart with its sharp teeth.

I howl with pain, but my cries go unheard.

The hooded figure walks away, wielding his scythe by his side back down the fiery road where we came. A low guttural growl from behind me yields the creatures' feast on me. A tail slithers on the ground worming its way to me like a snake and coils around what is left of my ankles.

A winged creature with horns like trumpets ascends over me. I cower, but I know my fate. Fireballs streak the sky, lighting the landscape like it's the 4th of July.

"Welcome to Hell," the Devil laughs.

"You're final resting place for eternity."

Shawnna Deresch has been crafting scary stories since she could first talk. Her love of horror began when she was a child watching horror movies with her father and now as an adult is obsessed with anything horror-related. She's a lover of paranormal investigations and loves checking out old cemeteries and old buildings. She lives with her three blue heelers and two black rescue cats in a condo near the beach of a big city. She is a member of the Horror Writers Association (HWA) and is the HWA Chicagoland Chapter Coordinator as well as an HWA Chapter Program Co-Manager. Her short stories have appeared in Kandisha Press Women of Horror Anthology Volume 3 and D&T Publishing ABC's of Terror, Volume IV. Shawnna can be found at: www.shawnnaderesch.com, Twitter: @shawnnaderesch, and Instagram: @shawnna_deresch_author. Her books can be found on Amazon.

"Of a Famished Tuesday at Idogogo"

Of a Famished Tuesday at Idogogo

By Jimoh Adeiza Abdulrahaman

O f a famished Tuesday: when Tarmacs were
thirsty for fluid, a car gyrated past me at Idogogo.
I heard the panegyrics of doom booming from its
stereo, and saw even a man behind the wheels
conjuring the grotesque beats.

{Sighs}

A man is an artist. Death is a ballerina.
tarmac is a stage. What happens when an artist
performs on a stage, conjuring tunes for a ballerina?

a serpent kills with a kisser
fire destroys in a flicker
gun kills with a trigger
but a car would mass murder}
With}

{Sighs}

swerve a}
FRSC ordered obedience from road users. but no
traffic rules here. no traffic signs. no yellow fever.

nothing. just a paved, hilly tarmac. what then could be
obeyed? nothing! so, a man descending a hilly tarmac,
phone against ear, was pressing the pedals and phoning
death. pee, pee, pee, I didn't hear. I saw a car but saw nothing
that swerved it.

{Sighs]

with a swerve off the tarmac onto the heart of
a Mechanic's shop, the car runs over bodies like
a mop wiping off stubborn stains from stairways.

A mechanic is a doctor and cars are the patients.
this car was a lunatic but the shop wasn't asylum.
there, I saw sick vehicles awaiting medication
but saw no mad vehicles, no madness at all.

{Sighs}

there came a rumble—of madness punishing innocence.
I saw Mechanics run to safety but yank back; bashed against a
rock, the car nosing further, profunding the cold embraces.

-arms - heads - legs $\times$ blood^1000 + my gasps

+crowd + gasps^100 - tranquility + 4×dead bodies.

{Sighs}

I saw a man disappearing. agile. swift and whole.
I couldn't believe a man would phone Death and Death
would pick up but won't converse with its caller.

a famished Tuesday drank deep. not water.
actually drank splattery blood. Sucker!

{Sighs}

A man is an artist. Death is a ballerina.
tarmac is a stage. What happens when an artist
performs on a stage, conjuring tunes for a ballerina?

a serpent kills with a kisser,
fire destroys with a flicker,
gun kills with a trigger,
but a car would mass murder}
with}

{Sighs}

swerve a}

Jimoh Adeiza Abdulrahaman is an Ebira-Nigerian creative and a student at ATBU, Bauchi. He's incurably obsessed with Adiche's Purple Hibiscus and Austin .J. Small's *The Man They Couldn't Arrest*. Abdulrahaman made the longlist for Abubakar Gimba prize for CNF in 2023 and his works have appeared in *SprinNG, Eboquills Our Girls anthology, Poetic Africa issue 10, 50 words stories,* and elsewhere.

When not writing or solving intimidating calculations, he can be found tweeting on X @JimohAbdul19.

"Ferryman's Fee"

The Ferryman's Fee

By Kelly Barker

P eople no longer placed an Obol under their loved one's
tongue after death. Which was Charon's fee for ferrying
the dead along the river Styx and Acheron to the
afterlife. The rivers had divided the realm of the living from
the Underworld since time began. However, the water was now
evaporating, making the riverbed ever more visible each day.
Like the gods, without people's prayers and belief, Charon and
the world as he knew it was fading.

Without barriers to separate life from death, the
worlds would collide into one and chaos would become the
new ruler—a faceless entity with no agenda. Still, he wasn't
ready to hang up his oars just yet, not even after many
millennia of service.

For the last thirty years, he had sat in his beached boat,
counting each bone in his once flesh-covered hand while
musing over what to do next. He needed to restore the people's
belief in him once more, and by doing so, restoring himself and

the gods to their former glory. A time when Pegasus flew across the skies into battle, when sailors feared the Kraken, and Medusa turned men into stone. Those were the days, he thought, sighing with appreciation.

However, Charon had only one skill, and that was taking passengers from one destination to another. After thirty more years, an idea finally presented itself. No longer would he need his oars or his boat. What he needed were a car and a driving license.

***

It had been four weeks since Holly had run down that jogger on the way back from work. She wasn't drunk, nor had she been driving dangerously. It was an accident, but her fight-or-flight response kicked in, making her speed away. Something far worse than the former. She had read on social media that the jogger died at the scene. She reread it a thousand times since, and on different platforms, hoping the information would miraculously change before her eyes. But the husband and father of three young children was not coming back from the body bag she had put him into.

Her phone rang, making her jolt with such force, a muscle pulled in her neck. Tears blurred her vision, so she couldn't see who was calling her from the screen of her phone. That being said, since she was no longer in employment, it could only be one person.

"Hi, Mum. I can't really talk at the moment—"

"Well, when can you talk? You've been acting so strange these last few weeks. You're making me and your dad worried. Please, just tell me what's wrong. Has someone hurt you—"

"No one has hurt me. I'm just upset because I lost my job, that's all."

"Rubbish. You were acting strange before you lost your job. Hence why you lost it."

"I don't know what to say. I'm looking for work, and once I've found something, I'm sure I'll be okay." Holly's tears of anguish flowed more freely than the ones from physical pain. She rubbed her pulled muscle while waiting for her mum's response.

"Drive up to Scotland," her mum said. "Come and stay with us for a few days."

"No, I can't."

Holly hadn't driven since that evening, which was why she'd lost her job. She hadn't turned up and didn't give an excuse as to why she wouldn't be coming in—not that she would have turned up even if she could walk to work. The guilt was eating her up. She'd lost sleep, weight, and so far had been successful in hiding that from her mum as well as not using her car.

"I don't want to drive up—"

"You won't have to. I'll order you a taxi."

The desperation Holly heard in her mum's voice broke her. She was hurting so many people, including her loved ones and herself. Her life was in tatters, rent was due on her home, and the bills were already piling up. She was certain it couldn't possibly get any worse than this, and that included going to prison. It was time to take control of the situation, and to do what she should have done at the time of the accident.

When she arrived in Scotland, she would tell her mum everything, then go to the nearest police station to hand herself in.

"Okay, Mum. Er, I'll organise a taxi to pick me up."

***

For whatever reason, Holly's taxi driver was driving a banged-up Rolls Royce, and wearing some sort of black bathrobe with the hood pulled up, concealing his face. She shook her head, unable to care any less at this point. If he was an axe murderer, so be it. Soon after she got in the back and clipped in her seatbelt, he pulled off her curb into the road without a word.

"Umm, sir, I told the taxi firm that this was a trip to Scotland. Is that okay with you? If so, I'll give you directions to my parent's house once we've crossed the border."

He said nothing.

Holly cleared her throat. "Excuse me, sir."

"We're not going to Scotland," the taxi driver said.

A combination of his hollow, yet heavily accented voice and the pink vehicle that had driven past made her heart stop, drop, then pound. She had called her go-to taxi company. A company run by women for women, who drove pink cars and didn't have any male drivers. Now a shadow of her former self, she had clearly dropped the ball.

"You don't work for Pink Angels, do you?"

"No, I don't."

"What's your name? What are you going to do to me? My mum's expecting me." She tried in vain to open the door.

"Modern-day mortals cannot pronounce my name to my liking, so you may call me the Ferryman. As for what I'm going to do to you, I need your belief in me, so I can continue doing what I have done for thousands of years, taking souls from one place to another." He kept his concentration on the road, never looking behind his shoulder. "Where your mum is concerned, she will be pleased to see you arrive early."

Maybe it was his calm demeanour or maybe it was because she no longer valued her life; whatever it was, she found her curiosity overriding her fear.

"The Ferryman? For thousands of years? You can't possibly believe you're a Greek myth. That's stupid."

"Ah, so you've heard of me, but you don't believe in me. Not to worry, by the time our journey ends, you will."

Holly didn't know how to respond, or whether she should, but since she was soon about to spend countless years behind bars, she thought she'd play along to take her mind off it. "Okay, Ferryman. I'm in. So how will you make me believe in what you're saying?"

"I'm going to open a portal to the Underworld and drive you along the river Styx. There, I will show you my boat and oar, and then I will watch the river water rise after your belief is restored."

"Why would my belief make the water rise?"

She listened intently while he told her what the world was once like and what would happen if there were no barriers between this life and the next. He spoke with an odd mixture of sadness and hope, continuously finding silver linings wherever he could, making her feel admiration for him.

171

When he stopped speaking, she looked out the window only to be greeted by a barren landscape. She jolted upright, used her sleeve to rub the glass, then shuffled across the seats to look out the other window. The river water looked black beneath the grey skies, and yet it somehow looked pure. The grass, too, appeared black, yet lush and pristine.

"We're here," he said.

"What the hell? This is impossible. Where are we, really? Hey, you, where are we?"

"I told you where I was taking you. Anyway, what do you think? Other than it being impossible, of course."

"I've lost my marbles. Wait... I have actually lost my marbles, and that's okay. I don't need them where I'm going, anyway. Just breathe."

The door locks clicked simultaneously.

"Shall we take a walk?" he said.

The first thing she did when she got out of the car was to see if the grass felt as soft as it looked. Then she followed the Ferryman to the water's edge. And true to his word, the water had receded by a considerable amount from the bank and downstream was a boat with the oars resting over the seat.

Holly looked up at him, then stepped around him to look under his hood. Her eyes deceiving her, she put one foot in front of the other, then stepped back. "Your... your face. Where is it?" Holly tripped backward.

With gloved hands, the Ferryman swept his hood back, revealing a scarcely fleshed skull without skin. "Don't be frightened. I said you would be with your mum shortly, and I meant it." He nodded his head toward the river. "At least I don't have to ask if you believe in me. The water is rising and I'm inching closer to becoming whole once more."

The Ferryman stood over her, holding his hand out. Holly looked from his feet to his face in quick concession, noting it was shock more so than fear she felt.

Taking his hand, she said, "I believe in you—I do. But what does this all mean? What do you want? For people to start putting coins over people's eyelids when they die?"

"The coins are called Obols and they are to be placed in the mouth under the tongue, not on the eyelids. You will tell people what you have seen here today, and you will make people believe in me. If you do not, the world as you know it will end."

"First, Obols are not in circulation. Second, no one would believe me. They would think I've gone mad."

"I have already brought countless people here and will continue to do so. The tide is turning even faster than I expected."

Holly sat down on the river bank, then crossed her legs. For the first time since she'd killed the jogger, she wasn't trapped in her mind thinking about what had happened on an endless loop. She had accepted that she'd go to prison, but now she knew for certain there was an afterlife, there was something she needed to know.

She was about to ask her question when the Ferryman surprised her by sitting and crossing his legs in the same way she was. He was sweet, she decided, but would she still feel that way once he answered her?

"Four weeks ago, I killed a man while driving back from work. Instead of stopping and calling an ambulance, I drove off." Whether it was because it was the first time she'd said it aloud, or because she'd used the exact words she'd rehearsed for when she handed herself in, tears of relief flowed down her cheeks. But would this feeling be short-lived? "You ferry the dead to either heaven, hell, or wherever they belong. When I die, and if I had your fee, where would you take me?"

The Ferryman closed his skinless eyelids. "After reading your thoughts, it's a tough one. Hell is mostly for the compassionless, the ones that take pride in their heinous acts, and you do not. However, your choice to drive off destroyed so many lives." He opened his eyes and looked down at her. "Let me ask you a question; if you could go back in time, what would you do differently?"

With the sleeve of her jumper, she wiped away her tears. "I would stop, get out of my car, and call the ambulance by his side while holding his hand. And I would do that because if he was conscious, he would know he wasn't alone, and that help was on its way. That's what I would do if I could go back in time."

"I know you would. Come with me." He stood and once again held his hand out for her to take. "It's time for you to go."

Taken aback by his abruptness, she took his hand, then followed him to his Rolls Royce. He opened the driver's door but didn't get in. When she tried to open her door, it wouldn't budge.

"Umm, I can't get in."

"You, Holly, are driving yourself back. Come on."

She stepped around the car to face him. "You don't understand. I don't drive anymore. I just can't."

"It's the only way you'll leave this place because I'm not driving you back." The Ferryman didn't have eyebrows, and yet Holly could sense them raised as if challenging her.

"You're my taxi driver. It's your job to take me back."

"My job is to ferry lost souls to their final resting place. Without my fee, I will take you to the realm between life and death—neither here nor there. Or... you can get in the car." He motioned her to step forward with his hands.

Initially, she shook her head, but she needed to see her parents one last time and hand herself in to the police. Plucking up the courage, she entered the car. Before she closed the door, she looked up at the Ferryman. "You didn't answer my question. You said it was a tough decision, but you didn't answer it."

"Keep driving along the river until you drive through the portal—"

"What portal? And why won't you give me an answer?"

"The portal—right there in front of you." He pointed at nothing.

"I can't see a bloody portal."

"That doesn't mean it's not there, does it?"

Holly looked over the steering wheel, then shrugged. "Whatever. If I get lost, you'll know where I'll be—which will be right back here."

"I have given you instructions to drive beside the river in a straight line. If you get lost, then the world is not worth saving."

For the first time in a long time, she smiled. "Okay, I can do this." She started the engine, then faced the Ferryman before he closed the door. "Although it's been a pleasure to have met you, I'm sure I'll just wake up tomorrow and think this was all a dream. But dream or not, I will still spread your message."

"The pleasure is all mine." He closed the door.

She inhaled deeply, then exhaled before driving forward. While looking out over the landscape, careful not to drive too close to the riverbank, she saw something from the corner of her eye. The black and silver interior was turning grey, and her CDs were sitting in the storage by the hand break.

"What the hell?"

While her hands were on the steering wheel, which belonged to her car, she noticed she was no longer wearing the green jumper she had put on that morning. Glancing down, she saw she was wearing her work uniform—a blue blazer and trousers.

Looking up, she recognised the road she was on, which was the route she'd taken from her previous place of employment to her home. "No, no, I can't relive this. Please, no."

She slowed right down, crawling along the road. A car beeped its horn from behind her, then overtook. When the car passed, its headlights illuminated the person who had haunted her day and night for four weeks. It was him—the jogger—the father of three.

The Ferryman was giving her a second chance, not only to do what she should have done in the first place but to save them both.

Shaking uncontrollably, she pulled over, next to the verge, and put her hazard lights on. "Why would you do this for me?" she said.

The answer was obvious. "Because you are a sweet, compassionate man."

Then her glove compartment crashed open. Coins trickled out. No, not just any coins. They were Obols. She laughed, then scooped up a handful. "Something tells me we're about to see a lot of these back in circulation."

With that, she slipped an Obol in her pocket and went home—back to her new old life.

Kelly Barker was born in Oxford and now lives in Witney with her husband and dog, Lana. She has been a barber for over twenty years and loves her job. However, reading and writing are her passion—a passion handed down to her by her great-grandmother, Isobel O'Leary.

You can find Kelly at:
www.kellybarker.org
https://www.facebook.com/kelly.m.barker.98
Twitter @MikeBar25891246
@Mikebar25891246

"The Dogwood Hotel"

The Dogwood Hotel

By Justin Sexton

*I*t was the summer of 1989. Arthur Anderson and his wife Cindy were patiently standing on a crowded curb in Times Square, New York. They observed the chaos around them as they tried desperately to wave down a taxi. The sun reflected off a giant skyscraper, blinding them both. They held their hands up to shield themselves from the hot sun.

Suddenly, a vibrant yellow cab pulled up beside them. They placed their luggage in the trunk and climbed into the back seat together. A gargoyle air freshener hung from the crooked and cracked rearview mirror. The taxi driver was tall and slender with a thick grey mustache. His skin was weathered and a black and white checkered hat sat perched on his unkempt hair. His cap hung low over his tired eyes and covered most of his worn face.

"Where are you headed?" he asked them.

"We are not sure, exactly. Our flight home to Boise was canceled due to bad weather on the West Coast. Some sort of bizarre lightning storm affecting the entire coast and inward. All flights out west are cancelled and all the hotels are booked solid because of the storm. We just need a place to stay for the night. Any suggestions?"

"The Dogwood Hotel has many rooms available. I can take you there," the driver suggested while puffing on a chubby cigar. The smoke was dense and excessive. It filled the vehicle and created a murky haze throughout the cab.

"Sure, that sounds great. Where is it?" Arthur inquired.

"It's on Long Island."

"Long Island? We aren't trying to go that far away from the city, but if there is nothing else available then that will have to do. What do you think, honey?" Arthur asked his wife. She glanced up from her book. Her bright blonde hair reflected in the rays of sunshine cascading through the dirty windshield.

"I just want a bed to sleep in tonight. I don't care where," she insisted.

"The Dogwood Hotel it is!" Arthur exclaimed.

"Perfect. My name is Abe," the driver mentioned as he ashed his cigar in a rusty tuna can nestled on the cluttered dashboard.

"Hi, Abe. I'm Arthur and this is my wife Cindy. We are visiting from Idaho. We came here for our honeymoon, just married."

Cindy nodded but remained quiet. She kept her focus on her novel as they drove. It took them a while to get out of the city but eventually, they were on their way out of town. The sun slowly descended as the taxi headed into Long Island.

Dusk approached and a full moon carefully took shape in the evening sky. An array of purple clouds and orange hues filled the heavens. Arthur and Cindy observed the countryside and the rustic cottages scattered beneath the sunset. The sound of traffic was replaced with the songs of birds, frogs, and summer insects. Their serenade was melodic and harmonious, a distant chorus, elusive and hypnotic. Native trees and dogwoods adorned the rustic neighborhoods scattered about.

The landscapes shuffled past the windows like a slide show. Off in the distance, a lighthouse peaked above the horizon.

"It's beautiful out here," Cindy stated as she stared out the taxi.

"Quiet, too," Arthur replied as he reached for his wife's hand and rubbed it gently.

"See the lighthouse? The hotel is just before it, on top of a cliff overlooking the ocean," Abe told them. He kept his eyes fixated on the road as he spoke.

"That sounds lovely," Arthur replied.

He smiled at his wife and she placed her book on the seat to admire the view. After a few minutes, Cindy noticed the vehicles parked in every driveway and traveling on the rural road were outdated.

"All the cars are old," she said abruptly.

"What do you mean?" Arthur asked.

"They are all from the 1930's. Why is that? Are we in Cuba?" she asked with a snicker. Abe laughed and nodded.

"Did you hear me? Abe, why the hell are all the cars from the 1930s?" she stated while pointing to an old Lincoln Continental parked outside a rustic bungalow.

"You're right, sweetheart. They all look like gangster cars," Arthur replied awkwardly.

"Abe, what's the deal? Are we on a movie set? Are they filming a mobster movie or something?" he asked the driver.

Abe glanced in the rearview mirror. "We're here," he grumbled.

"It sure is beautiful," Arthur whispered to his wife as he observed the lavender hotel perched on a foggy hill overlooking the ocean. Seagulls cried out overhead and the sun slowly sunk below the horizon. The lighthouse was neatly placed in the hotel's view.

"It's breathtaking!" Cindy exclaimed while observing the beautiful and elegant architecture. The building was three stories high and situated in the center was a tall six-story widow's peak with a clocktower. The roof was black with intricate thatching. The building was long and complex, the hotel wrapped around the cliff like a labyrinth.

"The hotel was built in 1920. It has a long, rich history," Abe told them while peering out the windshield.

"Thanks for the lift," Arthur mentioned as he paid Abe and offered him a generous tip. They retrieved their luggage from the trunk and waved goodbye to Abe. Arthur and Cindy peered up at the glorious craftwork. A chimera sat neatly perched on the edge of the widow's peak. Its face was fierce and unsettling.

"Weird," Cindy said when she saw the gargoyle's expression.

The couple walked into the empty lobby. It was charming and vintage throughout. The artwork and furniture were all from the 1930s. The space was warm and inviting.

They approached the front desk to purchase a room. The receptionist was short and robust. Her face pudgy and full of freckles. Her uniform was odd and outdated; Arthur looked around and saw all of the hotel staff were dressed in unique clothing.

"Even their outfits are vintage, this place is so cool. It's straight out of the Twilight Zone," Arthur said to his wife.

"It's like we passed through a portal to the 1930s," Cindy joked. She and Arthur laughed as they paid for the room.

"Number nine," the clerk muttered. A bellhop scurried over, decked out in old attire. His hat was worn and torn on the side. He was young with a red handlebar mustache. He was quiet and aloof, much like the front desk receptionist. The couple spotted the cast iron framed elevator and took it to the next floor. Old and rickety, it creaked and moaned as they ascended to the second level. The metal casing around the structure looked antique, artistic and elegant. The framework was slender and curvaceous like the hotel itself.

"I haven't seen one of these old elevators in years, this one is interesting," Arthur added as they reached the second floor. They stepped out of the elevator and followed the bellhop toward their room.

"Here it is. Number nine," Arthur said with a chuckle. The space was separated into several seating areas. It was painted maroon and beautiful gold. Chrome candles and lamps adorned the bedside. There was a living room with a small kitchenette alongside a full bathroom with a clawfoot tub.

"We serve dinner in the dining hall for all guests at five o'clock sharp. It is included in the price of the room. Tonight is chicken and eggplant parmesan," the bellhop stated before leaving.

The Andersons would not make it to dinner.

***

"This place is strange," Cindy mumbled while glancing out the window at the lush and vibrant garden in the courtyard.

"It's lovely and unique. I kinda like it," Arthur said as he kissed Cindy.

"Ever since we left the city, I haven't seen anything from our time let alone the last forty years. All the cars, clothing, architecture, and newspapers, are all outdated," she suggested as she held up the newspaper sitting on the coffee table by the couch. Cindy pointed to the date and headline.

"November 6, 1936. FDR wins! 4 More Years," Arthur replied while reading the paper.

"See!" Cindy shouted in a panic.

"It's a gimmick, they are trying to make the place seem old and vintage," he replied with a smirk.

"I doubt it, it was like that the whole drive here. It's odd," Cindy spat.

Just then, two purple 1929 Rolls Royce Phantom gangster cars swerved into the front of the hotel. Their tires squealed as they spun rapidly in the parking lot, creating razor marks on the pavement. Arthur and Cindy rushed to the window and watched as a man in a purple pinstripe suit got out of one of the cars and pulled out a Tommy machine gun. He began firing several rounds into a green Lincoln

Continental parked at the edge of the concrete near the courtyard. The driver was dead slumped over in the front seat with his head resting on the steering wheel.

"They just killed that man!" Cindy screamed.

"I'm sure it's a stunt, honey, part of the show," Arthur told her firmly. The newlyweds watched as the two gangsters rushed into the hotel. Gunshots rang out. Before they knew it the two men were in room nine. Their Tommy guns were pointed in Arthur and Cindy's faces. One man was tall and slender with long, bushy sideburns and the other was short and squatty. Their fedoras and pinstripe suits resembled the colors of ripened eggplant.

"I don't think this is an act," Cindy uttered in fear. The barrels of the machine guns were a couple feet from the brim of their noses. They could feel the heat lingering off the metal tips.

"You got us fellas. Nice show," Arthur said as he extended his hand to shake the men's hands.

"Make one more move and I'll shoot!" the fat guy shouted. A short, stubby cigar hung from his wide, chapped lips.

"You're coming with us!" the tall fellow yelled as he shoved Arthur and Cindy toward the door.

"On with it!" the tall gangster demanded. He pushed the weapon into Arthur's back and the four of them walked out of the room toward the stairs. Once they were out of the Dogwood Hotel, the two men bound and gagged them, forcing the couple into each of the Phantom's parked out front.

The cars were elegant and well-chiseled. The chrome grill and wide circular headlights were carefully carved and perfectly positioned on each vehicle. The cars were well-crafted, a true work of art. They were shiny and vibrant throughout. Each vehicle was decorated with a chimera hood ornament. The lion's face on both were delicately carved and polished. Its wings and tail were etched to perfection, much like the one on the widow's peak of the hotel. The men drove the Andersons to the other fork of Long Island. The drive took an hour and by the time they reached the dark and secluded forest the sun had set and the sky was obsidian,

"On the ground, both of you!" the short man howled.

"Please don't hurt us," Arthur begged. He clutched his wife tightly as they huddled on the wet ground.

"How did you get to the Dogwood Hotel? Who do you work for?" the tall and slender gangster demanded.

"We got a ride from Times Square in a taxi. The driver's name was Abe. We don't work for anyone. We are just visiting from Idaho," Arthur cried out while trembling with terror.

"Perfect," the slender mobster muttered. He held the machine gun firmly as he surveyed the forest shadows stretched behind the couple. Arthur and Cindy watched as an orb materialized out of thin air. It was round and pronounced. It was white and brightly illuminated as it shifted and undulated in the evening aether. The orb inched closer to the men looming over the Andersons.

"What on earth?" Cindy asked with bewilderment.

"Watch," the squatty mobster said in amazement.

The light pulsed and warbled before it stretched open. A creature with an elongated body stepped out of the illuminated object. The being's face was grey and muted. Its eyes were turquoise and entrancing. Its head was abnormal and well-rounded with a triangle between its two big eyes. The creature's torso was tight and muscular. The rest of its body was emaciated and malnourished. It seemed alien-like as it opened its small-rimmed mouth and spoke.

"I see you brought me two more." The creature's voice was robotic and synthetic, it resembled the sounds of a synthesizer.

"We took them from the Dogwood Hotel," the chubby gangster told the elongated entity.

"Just as I ordered," it stated before placing its slender fingers on Arthur and Cindy's heads. Their eyes shifted and swiveled in extreme rotation. Both bodies convulsed and trembled violently on the wet earth. The group watched as energy from the forest appeared in every corner of the dense thicket.

The greenwood was eerie and ominous as a mysterious vapor filled the forest. It was purple and hypnotizing. The mist was pungent and lingered through the trees. Both men plummeted to the ground in prayer. The forest fell silent as the strange substance floated toward the couple slowly. The vapor entered Arthur and Cindy through their nostrils. Their bodies drifted from limp and dormant to active and awake. They both stood erect and opened their eyes wide. They looked around and examined the forest before bowing to the creature and joining the men in prayer. They all spoke in tongues while holding their third eye against the forest floor.

Several figures appeared in the shadows of the woods. People in vintage and modern attire began walking toward them carrying lanterns and singing. The mob consisted of twenty people wielding old books and antique oil lamps. The men wore black collared shirts and they each had long beards. The women wore lavender dresses with black triangles strategically placed on them.

They formed a circle around the creature and a well-dressed man in a pinstripe suit and tie with a purple fedora entered the circle. He sprinkled salt on the ground in the shape of a pentagram. The process was methodic and well-calculated.

All of a sudden, a portal opened above the geometric design. It was small and shaped like a triangle. As it grew, various demons and dark entities climbed out of the vortex and into the surrounding New York greenwood. Some were dark and grotesque while others looked like regular humans. A couple that resembled Arthur and Cindy stepped foot into the wilderness. They appeared curious and childlike as they observed their new realm. The clones scampered off into the darkness to replace the Andersons in real life. Once everyone vanished, the couple was alone in the forest with the mobsters and the creature.

"They have been mutated. Bring them back to the base," the entity directed.

The men loaded the couple into each of the Phantom cars and headed back to the Dogwood Hotel. During the drive, parts of Cindy's true self began to surface. The mutation spawned by the creature didn't fully take. Cindy was wading between lunacy and self-identity. Once they returned to the hotel, the Andersons followed the men to the basement. The four of them entered the iron-framed elevator and descended underground. The journey was long and secluded. They traveled deep beneath Earth's surface.

When they reached the bottom, the elevator doors opened and revealed a giant, ancient cave. It was massive and spacious. The room was dark and dank. Small torches were scattered about and their light flickered to create moving shadows that danced on the walls of the cavern

The area was full of people in red cloaks deep in prayer. They were hunched around an altar with a cage beside it. Trapped inside was a creature that looked different than the one in the forest. They were similar in shape and form but this creature's skin was blue instead of grey. It was screaming in agony as the people continued to chant in bizarre tongues around it. It spat and hissed at the crowd as foam flung from its gaping mouth, gnashing its sharp and rigid teeth. A man in a black hood carrying a tattered book approached the altar. Hanging above the shrine was a giant pentagram. It was black and distinct. Animal skulls and human bones decorated the elaborate sacrificial stone before it. The man in the black hood observed the crowd and spoke.

"Greetings followers, thank you for joining me tonight. Some of you have come from far away to be here this evening. You journeyed from your homes, through the tunnels hidden deep beneath them. You made the trek under the earth, so you could take part in this sacred ritual."

The audience was captivated as the priest continued his sermon. "I present to you our sacrifice for this evening. This demon was captured by the Dogwood Hotel staff last night. We are forever grateful for our partnership with the hotel. Over the last ten years, they offered us a safe place to meet and perform our rituals in secrecy. Here, tonight, we have several famous musicians and movie stars. We also are honored to be alongside several politicians and private investment bankers. Thank you for joining us and we are happy to have you in attendance this evening. We will now begin the sacred ritual."

The man in the black hood removed the creature from the cage. It yelled and fought as several members in cloaks pinned the entity on the altar and tied it to the platform. The priest in the black hood lifted a giant stake and said a prayer before he plunged the dagger directly into the creature's chest. It screamed in pain, then it collapsed and fell quiet. After it squirmed for a few moments it stopped moving. The entity was lifeless as blood poured from its strange and abnormal body.

"Take a sliver and live forever!" the leader called out. All at once the followers ran toward the corpse and started eating it. They ripped into the creature's skin and tore its abdomen apart. Bits of flesh hung from their blood-stained teeth as they devoured the creature bit by bit. Arthur took several bites of the demon's flesh and smiled at his wife. Cindy did not partake.

After a couple of minutes, the being was gone and his bones were tossed on the altar. Then the priest began to sing, "Take a sliver, live forever. Take a sliver, live forever!"

Cindy watched the scene unfold, she was petrified. Her true self was surfacing and peering through the subtle cracks.

"Arthur we have to get out of here," she whispered.

He ignored her and continued to chant with the group. "Take a sliver, live forever."

His eyes were black and he appeared to be in a trance. The singing continued for several measures before it finally ended. The ritual seized and the crowd quickly dispersed. The two gangsters stepped out of the elevator and grabbed Cindy and Arthur.

"Back to ground level," the skinny man directed.

Once they were back at the hotel, Cindy and Arthur were taken to a section designated for the Dogwood staff.

"You will live here and work as hotel staff like the rest of us," the squatty mobster mentioned while puffing on a mangled cigar.

"Please, you must let us go, we just want to go home," Cindy pleaded. The men stared at her with confusion.

"She didn't mutate," they both said simultaneously.

"What do we do?" the fat guy asked.

"I don't know this has never happened before. We need to get her back to the forest," the one with sideburns suggested.

"We don't have time for that! Arthur kill your wife!" the fat one yelled. In an instant, Arthur lunged at his bride and grabbed her by the neck. He lifted her off the ground and clenched his fingers deep into her throat. She began to lose consciousness. Cindy fell to the wooden floor below. Her body made a loud thud when it hit the solid oak ground.

"Is she dead?" the skinny fellow asked.

"I think so. Let's tie her up and throw her in the ocean," the other man replied.

They wrapped Cindy in a rug with several weights attached to hold her down and rolled her toward the cliff.

Then men shoved her over the edge and watched her plummet into the Atlantic.

"That should do it!" the stout one proclaimed as they retreated to the hotel.

Cindy awoke under the ocean to find herself wrapped in the rug. She fought tirelessly to break free. Once she did, she managed to swim to shore. She saw a road in the distance and ran toward it. A cab approached her and she flagged it down immediately. Cindy rushed over to the passenger door.

"Help me, two men tried to kill me at the Dogwood Hotel!" she shouted. It was then she recognized the driver, it was Abe.

"I remember you miss, get in. I will help," Abe hollered as he reached for the door and shoved it ajar.

Cindy stepped in the taxi and they high-tailed it to the hotel. When the cab pulled up everything was different. The building was modern and futuristic. There was no chimera perched on the widow's peak and the staff was dressed in regular attire. Cindy rushed around the lobby in a panic. She spotted the elevator and ran to it, Abe followed her closely. It was silver and up to date. She went inside and ascended to the second floor. She rushed down the hallway and clasped the door knob to room nine in her trembling hand. She ripped the door open and tumbled inside. The room didn't match her memory. The walls were purple instead of maroon. The wallpaper in the kitchenette was brand new. It was green with purple eggplants on it.

"What the hell? Everything is different," she muttered.

"You crossed through the portal and back somehow," Abe suggested while he reached for his book of matches. He removed one and struck it against the matchbook. He lit his cigar and took a giant puff.

"What portal?" she asked.

"The one we drove through to get here. It's controlled by the mob. We must have traveled into it when I took you to the hotel the first time and somehow you crossed back to 1989.

"So that means Arthur is trapped in 1936?" she asked.

"I'm afraid so my dear," Abe replied.

"I don't understand. How is this possible?"

"I can explain. I was born on Long Island and have been a cab driver in the city for many years. In 1933 there were two gangs at war in New York City. Murdock's Mob and the Green Gangsters. Murdock's Mob was comprised of Frank Murdock and his gang of men in purple pinstripe suits. They ran the prostitution rings and controlled most of the bootlegging on Long Island. They would still liquor deep in the woods after midnight. They tailored their shoes to resemble animal hooves so they couldn't be detected by law enforcement. Legend has it that one evening while they were bootlegging they stumbled upon a satanic cult performing a sacrificial ritual in the middle of the forest.

The mobsters watched as the Satanists opened a dark and demonic portal in the center of the woods. A giant orb appeared and an elongated creature stepped out of the vortex and presented himself to the leader and his followers. Murdock and his gang were mesmerized. They struck a deal with the Satanists and a partnership was formed between the two.

With the demon and the satanic cult on the Murdock's side, they were able to obliterate the Green Gang with ease. In a matter of months, Frank and his mob-controlled all of New

York City and Long Island. The cult allowed the gangsters to utilize their demons and join their group as followers. In turn, Murdock and his crew provided a safe place for the Satanists to worship underground and even helped to recruit infamous members. They continued to pray and practice their rituals in secrecy. One night while summoning evil spirits, they created a riff in time. Because of this, time here fluctuates rapidly. Murdock and his crew control the portal like a mechanical gadget they can turn on or off. I don't understand how you made it back to 1989, however," Abe told Cindy.

"So, how do we get back to 1936 and bring my husband home?" Cindy asked reluctantly.

"We don't," he stated firmly.

"We can't just leave him," Cindy argued.

"You will be together again soon," Abe demanded.

"How?"

"Just like this," Abe whispered as he reached for his weathered skin and peeled back his flesh to expose his demonic figure. His face was grey and disfigured. He grew tall and hunched over Cindy. He wrapped his slender fingers around her porcelain neck and smiled exposing its blood-stained teeth.

In one swift motion, the demon snatched Cindy and attacked her violently. He ripped into her stomach and gouged at her face. The demon ate every bit of Cindy, leaving behind only her bones for the altar. When he was finished, the creature shapeshifted back into a New York cab driver.

Abe hopped in his yellow taxi and headed back to the city singing,

"Take a sliver, live forever. Take a sliver, live forever."

Justin Sexton is an author, musician, and podcaster living in the mountains of north Georgia. He finds inspiration for his work in folklore, old-school horror movies, life experiences, and nature.

He currently has a novella "The Nomad" out and another novella "Mirror Island" coming out summer 2024 through Above the Rain Collective.

"In Death, As in Life"

In Death, As in Life

By Juliet Rose

L aura yawned as the last of the children climbed off the bus and she slid the door shut. They waved as they walked toward their front door, their multi-colored backpacks bobbing on their small frames. She raised her hand back and forced a smile through her tired lips. She loved being a bus driver but sometimes the days got long. Too long. At least this day was over and she could park the bus by her house and put her feet up.

Twenty years of driving a school bus. She always thought it would be temporary until she got her shit together and got a real job. But weeks turned into months, months into years, years into decades.

She eased the bus out of the neighborhood and headed for her tiny farmhouse outside of town. As she left the outskirts, she drove by the cemetery and grimaced. Her mother had recently passed and she hadn't made it out to her grave since the burial. Guilt seized her chest and she slowed the bus as she neared the entrance. Maybe just a quick stop. Make sure her mother's grave was tidy.

She stopped the bus on the main cemetery road and hiked in to visit her mother's grave. Faded silk flowers drooped near the headstone, a reminder of the time that had passed. Laura signed and plucked the now pale pink and purple flowers out of the holder and clutched them to her chest.

"Sorry, Mom."

Silence greeted her and she glanced around at the other headstones. One was covered in bright colorful flowers and teddy bears. Laura wandered over to them and her heart fell when she saw the age. Nine years old. A little girl named Beatrice. Even though the child had died almost thirty years ago, the flowers were fresh and the teddy bears looked like they had just come off the store shelf. Laura leaned down and let her finger trail down the side of one of the bears. It was soft, not yet weathered from sitting out there.

Laura plucked a single flower off one of the stems and stood up, carrying it to her mother's grave. She set it on top of the headstone and stared, tears welling up in her eyes. Her mother had been her biggest supporter and her best friend. She thought they'd have years together but her mother dropped dead in the grocery store of an undiagnosed heart condition at sixty-three. Laura had only turned forty herself right before her mother's death. They'd had a big party for the big 4-0, as her mother said.

Laura let the tears fall and regretted her choices in life. She'd never found the one, never had children of her own. Perhaps that's why she remained a bus driver. She got to hear the laughter and chatter of children five days a week. In the summer, she drove a smaller bus for summer camp field trips.

At the end of the day, she was alone. She didn't mind most times, but since her mother's death, the nights and weekends seemed to drag on and on. She had a brother but he'd left their small town after high school, married, and moved, of all places, to Costa Rica. They weren't close anymore, and she only heard from him during the holidays and on her birthday.

She turned and squinted around the cemetery. Once those were all living people with families, hopes, dreams, plans for the future. Now they lay in the cold dark for eternity. Maybe. She wasn't religious or even spiritual, so death seemed pretty final. No signs from her mother, no grand release to streets of gold. Sadness gripped her heart, hoping she was wrong. She didn't want to think this hole in the ground was the end of her mother.

She wandered back to the bus and climbed through the still-open doors. Sitting in the driver's seat, she slowly drew the doors close and wiped the tears off her cheeks. She was still alive but didn't feel like it. She took one more glance at her mother's grave as she drove away and the thought of digging her mother up to hug her one more time crossed her mind. It gave her a weird comfort. She shook it off and pulled out of the cemetery, heading for home.

Movement in the large mirror above her head caught her eyes and she gasped, jerking her head around. Nothing was there. She frowned and rubbed her head. The cemetery must have given her the heebie-jeebies even though it didn't make her feel that way. She found it peaceful. She peered in the mirror again, greeted by nothing but empty seats.

As she rounded the bend heading toward her house, lost in her thoughts, a strange sound came from the back of the bus. She slowly turned her head, expecting to see nothing as the sound erupted again. A giggle. It sounded like a giggle. She ran through the children she took home on her bus and was sure they'd all gotten off.

"Who's back there?" she asked, expecting to be greeted with silence.

Another giggle.

As her head rotated to the back, she saw something in the last row. A girl, standing by the back door. Laura almost drove off the road and whipped back around to face the front, grabbing the steering wheel tightly. She was seeing things. Maybe it was a jacket or a book bag. She pulled off to the side of the road and took a deep breath before turning back around. Nothing was there. No girl, no backpack, no book bag.

"Get it together," she whispered to herself. "Why would a child still be on the bus?"

"I want to go home," a voice behind her said and Laura couldn't help but scream.

She jumped out of the seat and spun toward the back. A young girl was standing in the middle of the aisle. Not a little girl she knew. Her dress was older and she was holding a small bear. Laura's mouth dropped open as she seriously considered if she was losing her mind. She stood frozen by the driver's seat and stared, not sure what to do. The little girl cocked her head, her eyes not blinking.

"Take me home, please."

"H-home? I don't understand. Who are you? How did you get on my bus?" Laura asked, her voice tight and high.

"I am Beatrice, my mama calls me Bea."

Beatrice? Like the girl's headstone at the cemetery? Laura placed her hand on the steering wheel to steady herself and shook her head. "Where did you come from? You can't just get on buses, little girl. Your parents must be sick with worry. Do you go to Long Creek Elementary?"

The girl turned her head in confusion. "No, ma'am. I go to Daniels Elementary."

Daniels Elementary? That school had been closed for as long as Laura had been a bus driver. Someone was playing a prank on Laura and not a very funny one. She sat down and rested her head against the steering wheel. What was she supposed to do with this child? Did the child see her looking at Beatrice's grave and decide to pull a fast one on her?

If so, she must have someone else playing along. Laura wondered if they were on the bus, as well. She jumped up and headed for the back of the bus. Beatrice, or whatever her name was, was gone. Laura checked each seat but there was no sign of the girl or anyone else.

Laura sat on one of the seats and began to bawl. Losing her mother must have sent her over the edge. She had to admit, she'd not let herself grieve or truly come to accept her mother was no longer there. She must have visualized the child in response to missing her own mother. After all, she'd just seen a grave with the name Beatrice on it. Accepting her mind was cracking, Laura got up and went back to the driver's seat, making it home without any more incident.

"I miss you, Mama," she whispered as she pulled the bus into her driveway. "Sorry, I haven't visited. It's just... it's just not you there. I want the *you* here."

She climbed off the bus and went inside her dark house. Her cat Simpson wound his way around her ankles and purred. At least she had him. She scooped him up and went to the kitchen to make herself a sandwich before she committed to watching television the rest of the evening. She set Simpson down by the sink and poured him a bowl of water with a scratch on his head. "There you go, boy."

Once her sandwich was made, she wandered to the living room and plopped down on the couch. Half the time she fell asleep there watching television and she felt like this was going to be that kind of night. The TV droned on for hours and she felt her eyes getting heavy. She considered relocating to her bed but decided there wasn't much difference either way. Simpson climbed up beside her and curled next to her ribcage as she gave in to sleeping on the couch.

Later she was woken up by the sound of Simpson growling and rubbed her eyes. He was staring at the corner of the room. Laura could make out a shadow and sat up. It was the girl. Beatrice. Laura put her hand on Simpson who was clearly perturbed about the visitor. The girl seemed distraught and Laura couldn't help but feel for this apparition.

"Why are you here?" she asked, knowing in her heart why.

"I want to go home," the girl replied.

Home.

Laura decided to play along. "Where is home?"

The girl scrunched up her face, then shrugged. "It's a white house, with black shutters. My mama planted rose buses all around the house. It has a white fence out front."

Laura sighed. That wasn't much to go off of. The girl went to Daniels Elementary. "Did you ride the bus to school?"

The girl shook her head. "I walked with other children."

Close enough to walk. Okay. "Why do you want to go home? Aren't you... uh, are you dead?"

The girl frowned, then nodded. "I guess so."

"How did you get on my bus?"

"I saw it at the cemetery. There aren't many children to play with there. I thought if I got on, you'd take me to school. Or home."

So if Beatrice was really there, she was a ghost. She saw Laura at the cemetery and got on the bus. Laura knew it all sounded crazy but decided to go with it. "Did you ever ride the bus when you were in school?"

Beatrice nodded. "Yes, to stay at friend's houses or for field trips."

Laura stroked her temples. In order to get Beatrice to go away, she needed to get her home. A thought occurred to her. "Is your mama still alive?"

Beatrice smiled. "She comes to my grave every day." Her face darkened and her shoulders dropped. "I need to get home. She needs me there to come over."

Come over? Oh. Her mother was dying and she wanted to be there to guide her on. Laura couldn't believe she was even considering it. She got up and grabbed her keys off the hook, setting Simpson down on the floor. Either she was losing her mind and about to go searching for a house in the dark, or she wasn't and would bring Beatrice home.

She slipped on her shoes by the door and glanced over to see if Beatrice was still there. The girl was and followed her out the door. As they made their way onto the bus, Laura saw Simpson hop up in the window of the house. He was not happy being disrupted from sleeping next to her. She fired up the bus and drove toward the old elementary school. The abandoned school was even creepier in the dark and Laura could imagine children playing on the now dilapidated playground. She paused by the school and turned to Beatrice.

"Do you remember which way you walked home?"

Beatrice lifted her hand and pointed to the right of the school. Laura followed her direction and they crept through the night in search of the home. At times, Beatrice seemed confused but then would point Laura in the direction she should go.

They went a couple of blocks when Beatrice whispered, "Stop."

They were on a dark road and Laura couldn't see a house. She worried maybe she'd been lured out on false pretenses and whoever, or whatever, Beatrice was might murder her. She squinted out the side windows and could make out what looked to be an old driveway. Beatrice was staring down the thin trail and nodded.

"Down there."

Laura felt the hair on her neck rise and questioned if she should go that way. She'd heard stories of people using children to lure unsuspecting people to their deaths. She shook her head. "I don't think so."

"Please. Do you have a mama?" Beatrice asked.

Laura watched her for a moment, then dropped her head. "No. Not anymore. Her grave is next to yours."

Beatrice tipped her head. "Oh. You must be sad. I miss my mama. I want to be with her. Don't you want to be with your mama?"

Oh, how Laura did. She'd give about anything to see her again. She put the bus in gear and turned down the overgrown driveway. No lights led their way and she struggled to stay on the path. They came up to an old rundown house. Maybe it had once been white with black shutters with a white fence. Now, it was faded, gray, with a few remaining peeling shutters. A small dented car sat in the driveway, but no sign of life existed anywhere around.

"Is this it?" she asked Beatrice.

Beatrice clutched her bear and bobbed her head. "Mama's inside."

"Do you want me to go in with you?"

"No, Ma'am. She's waiting for me. It's time." Beatrice went down the stairs as Laura opened the door. She turned back to face Laura and smiled. "You're mama wants you to know she is always with you. She watches out for you. She says, 'Pay attention to the little things'."

Laura nodded but wasn't sure she believed Beatrice. She wasn't sure she believed a ghost child she'd driven to an old house in the middle of the woods. She chuckled at herself and winked at Beatrice. "Go see your mama, I know she will be so happy to hold you again."

Beatrice clambered off the bus and practically ran to the front door, stopping to wave back at Laura like all the children did when they went home. Laura raised her hand and shut the door tightly, fighting back tears. She waited until Beatrice got to the door and opened it, disappearing inside. Laura waited, expecting something big to happen, but the house remained dark and quiet.

She turned the bus around and headed back out of the driveway, wondering what really just happened. As she came to the main road, she felt something come over her and peered back at the house. Two orbs rose from the chimney and danced in the sky above the house. Laura knew Beatrice was back with her mama. For eternity. Sadness washed over her as she thought of her own mother and how she didn't know how to reach her.

The orbs came down the road and moved around the bus as she drove. They were thanking her. She could feel their gratitude, but her heart was heavy. She wanted what they had. As she neared home, the orbs disappeared and she wished them a safe journey. At least she had Simpson. She eased up to her house and cut the engine, wondering how she'd be able to get up in the morning and do it all over again. Pick up other people's children, bring them home to their families, then go back to her solitary life. She wanted more.

As she got off the bus, she stopped and stared up at the sky. "Mama, are you there?"

The stars twinkled but no response came. She felt such loneliness it was hard to breathe. She envied Beatrice for being able to reconnect with her mother and only wished the same for herself. Maybe she could do it. Find a way. Tears streamed down her cheeks as she considered the option of ending her life on that plane of existence. Simpson jumped in the window and she knew she couldn't do that to him. Leave him all alone. She wiped her face and headed for the door when three orbs shot out of the sky toward her, dancing around her. She knew one was Beatrice and one was Beatrice's mother, what was the third?

As if answering her question, the orb came to her and rested on her chest. All the love and support she'd ever felt in her lifetime filled her soul and she knew. Beatrice and her mother were giving her the only thanks they knew how.

"Hello, Mama," Laura whispered as she cupped her hands around the orb. It vibrated back at her. "I miss you."

The orb slipped inside her chest and told Laura all the things she needed to hear. She wasn't alone. She didn't need to live in solitary confinement. It was time to truly live and stop hiding from the world. Her mother was always with her and wanted her to live. The orb came out and joined the other two. Laura watched as they faded into the night sky. Once they were gone, she stayed outside under the stars, allowing the message to sink in.

The following day she gave her notice at work, packed up her house and Simpson, and set out on a journey to make her life worth living. With her mother in her heart and by her side.

There was no going back.

Juliet Rose is a multi-award-winning cross-genre author in contemporary fiction, visionary suspense, sci-fi realism, and supernatural horror. She is adept at blending genres and challenges both herself and the reader to think outside of their comfort zone by introducing new ideas into familiar tropes. She has ten published fiction books. In her free time, she also dabbles in magazine and anthology writing. While she resides in the mountains of Georgia, she's lived all over the United States and Mexico, using these experiences in her writing.

Her website is authorjulietrose.com and includes all of her social media links and contacts.

"A Ride to Remember"

A Ride to Remember

By Martin Eastland

"**C**AN IT NOW!" Carole yelled over her shoulder. More quieter, under her breath, she continued, "At least till we get there."

It had been a long drive and she was shattered. The girls in the back - her daughters - were acting up again.

Can't blame 'em, really, she thought. Maine's a long way off, way too far in to turn back home to Sidewinder. They had cooled off a bit now and were immersed in their iPads. One twelve, the other six, she hated herself for letting them this close to the outside world. That crap was for adults.

"Too many predators online these days," would be her excuse, and she would be right, too.

There were those 'to catch a predator' tv shows on re-run, and it had scared the shit out of them. That was before the divorce she instigated, citing "irreconcilable differences."

"Fuckin' around with the bitch ass blonde next door," she had retorted. Or at least that's what she had begun to suspect. The rain was battering on the roof, cascading down the windshield only to be spread over it by the wipers.

A light came into view, and she heaved a sigh of relief. As she took the right exit into the parking lot, the welcome sight of the Golden Arches lit the interior of the car.

She pulled up in front and turned to face the girls. "Momma's gonna go get some chow. Sit here quietly, and don't move. I'll be a coupla minutes, tops. I'm locking the door, so you should be fine."

The girls nodded, still immersed in their phones. She got out of the car and found the rain had stopped. She looked around and made sure no one saw her, then activated the car alarm. The girls looked up, watching her walk to the entrance. Returning to their own world, they zoned out again.

Something is wrong out there, she thought as she stood inside watching the car intently. She could see no movement inside it, just two motionless forms.

They're good girls, she thought to herself. The server called to her and she walked over to the counter, picking up her order. Smiling, she took it and walked briskly to the door where a young man held the door for her. Shyly, she smiled at him in thanks. His good looks weren't wasted on her.

Shit! If I were ten years younger, you wouldn't have a prayer! she mused. She began to laugh inwardly as she walked to the car. Pushing the car alarm, she opened the door, put the bag on the passenger seat, and returned to full height. She stiffened, her face pale, as a low, guttural voice spoke from her waist.

"They die if you make a sound. Gimme the keys right now!"

Terrified, she handed them over. He stood up quickly and walked around to the other side.

"Get in," he said, and she complied. He got in and closed the door. He handed her the keys.

"Drive."

Trying to remain calm for the girls' sake, her high-pitched, hoarse voice squeaked, "Where to?"

He looked in the right-hand side wing mirror, distantly answering her, "Just get us outta here, lady. Head for I-95, and I'll tell you what from there."

She pulled out into traffic, the journey into her nightmare about to begin...

***

THE RAIN HAD been hammering against the car for the last half hour, and the silence was excruciating. She could see he was staring absently out of the side window. He was looking at her via reflection, but she wouldn't know that. She reached under her seat, fumbling around, trying not to attract his attention.

He turned to face her, opening his jacket. He flashed her own pistol at her, a .38 Smith & Wesson, snub-nosed. He glared at her, impassive and distant, his eyes vacant rooms. He spoke, his voice calm yet cold, droning.

"This what you're lookin' for?" he asked.

She looked away, biting her lip, waiting for his next move. Instead, he closed his jacket, returning his steely, frozen eyes toward the passing traffic.

"Take the next exit. There's a 7/11 just after it," he instructed.

She saw the off-ramp, taking the lane leading to it.

Carole Hardin was not, by any stretch, a stupid woman. She had graduated in the top 2% of her class and had achieved a lot since then. But that had all changed when her firstborn came along. She had found herself married to her boyfriend, and it had been good for the first two years, sliding off after that.

What the hell, she had conceded ever since. *You weren't the grand prize, either!*

Now, where was she? Heading east for two thousand-plus miles let her girls see the father she had cut out of the picture out of sheer petulance.

The lights of the 7/11 forecourt appeared, and she pulled in.

"Park it over there," he instructed. She drove the car into the vacant spot at the far end of the lot and turned off the engine.

He turned to her, head-on. "Alright, here's what's happenin'. The munchkin's comin' to the store wit' me. It's major league snack time. My treat. One warning, only. Anything goes down, she dies first," he said, indicating the youngest daughter, Hallie. Her sister, Samantha, had just turned twelve a few months before.

"You want anything?" he asked.

She stared at him, choked, and unable to vocalize much of a reply.

"I'll get you somethin' for the trip. Let's go, sweet stuff!"

Hallie looked at her mother, unsure of what she should do. Carole hated it but forced the words out. "It's ok, Hallie. Be happy when you go in there, okay?"

Hallie nodded and opened the rear door, getting out. The creep opened his door, stepping onto the concrete. He took her hand and walked to the entrance. Hallie looked back at the car. Her mother and Samantha were watching, fearing for her.

Half-relieved, Carole heaved a sigh and watched as he entered the gas station with her. *At least he hadn't disappeared with her*, she thought. Having said that, she considered he could easily sneak out of there with her daughter without them seeing them.

The following ten minutes were absolute torture for Carole, lifting her cell phone to her eyeline so that she wouldn't miss anything by looking down at it. Movement caught Samantha's eye and she shook her mother's right shoulder. Carole whipped her eyes up to him.

The image would remain with her forever.

He was walking toward the car, smiling. *A nice smile, too,* she thought, despite herself. He carried a large bag of snack food in one hand and Hallie wrapped around his neck, laughing happily. Her heart skipped a beat as she looked on, the sight of her potential rapist bonding with her daughter.

It wasn't as far-fetched as she thought, as they had no inkling of his eventual intentions once she had taken him where he wished to go. She had to accept that it was a contentious possibility. It could well be only a matter of time before he...

She shook the image from her mind as he opened the rear door, letting Hallie get in with Samantha, handing her the bag before closing the door, walking around to the passenger side, reclining his seat. He handed her the keys and gestured for the exit. The engine turned over, and the car pulled out of the forecourt, headed out to the interstate and I-95, Maine-bound.

***

THEY HAD TAKEN the wrong turn and ended up on a deserted country road. His agitation was rising, but he kept it in check for the kids' sake.

Samantha looked in the rearview mirror and saw a glint of movement. But there were no headlights on if it even was a car behind. A thought occurred to her. Biting her lip, she finished her banana, rolling down her window. Feeling the sudden blast of cold, damp air, he turned, staring at her with those lifeless eyes again.

"What? I want some fresh air, alright?"

He turned to face the road, and with a deft move, her eyes on the jerk the whole time, she flicked the banana skin out over her head. She prayed it was what she believed it to be. Seconds later, the car was lit up by the red, white, and blue lights of a Sheriff's Department squad unit, its siren piercing and loud.

The creep didn't budge an inch as she had expected, having heard the cops. Carole almost cried at the release of it.

"What do you want me to do, now?" she inquired. He didn't seem to care about getting caught.

"Pull over," he purred.

She pulled the car over and rolled down the window. He watched the Sheriff get out of his car, followed by his deputy, Norm, and put the gun under the seat, ready for use. The Sheriff arrived at the window and tapped it.

Carole rolled it down. "Was I speeding, Officer?"

"No, ma'am," he said.

"What did I do?" she asked him.

"We were on our way to the all-night deli when all of a sudden, this falls outta the sky," he said, sternly. He held up Samantha's errant banana skin in the air with two fingers.

"We don't cotton to litterbugs in these heah parts, ma'am! Y'all step out the cah, now, y'heah? You and your kids can talk to my associate heah, and I'll talk to yo' husband for a few ticks. Go on, now."

The creep didn't move an inch. He had a gut feeling it was the end of the road. *Let's just see what happens*, he mused to himself. Maybe – just maybe the old-timer would just give her a ticket or a warning or whatever.

As soon as the kids and Carole had been safely deposited in the rear of the squad unit, the deputy, Norm, returned to the Sheriff's side.

"Y'all mind showin' me yo license and registration fo' second," he asked, thinly smiling a humoring smile.

"You'll have to ask the lady. She's got the papers in her purse. She's just givin' me a ride to Lewiston."

Wade Miller had been a lawman for the last thirty years, from as far out as Texas and the Florida swamps, and a few places in between. He knew bullshit when he heard it and looked at Norm. It was a code between them, a silent order. Norm pulled his gun out quickly, as the Sheriff stood back.

"Get yo' ass out of the cah, butter cheeks!"

The creep got out of the car, standing in front of the open door, blocking it. Miller proceeded cautiously. This was a slippery little sum'bitch. He frisked the stranger down, standing back as he spun him around to face him.

"Listen hahd, son...we gonna be takin' y'all down the station house to take a lil' pop quiz. In the meantime, I'm arrestin' you under suspicion of abduction. We'll come up with more after we sort this horse shit out."

The man made a grab at Miller's holster, and Norm shot him twice in the chest. He slid down the rear passenger door, holding his wounds, his eyes incredulous. He collapsed in a heap at Norm's feet. The Sheriff motioned for Norm to return to the kids and Carole. He walked away, and Miller took a good, hard stare at the stranger. Almost sneering, he turned and headed for his car.

He was five feet from the squad car when Carole jumped up, her face panicked, and screamed out, "NOOO!"

The Sheriff saw Norm pulling his gun out. He cursed under his breath, turning on a dime (despite his proud South-Western gut) to see the once-dead stranger bearing down on him, gun pointed. Without hesitation, the adrenaline rushed through him, as he put five shots, perfectly grouped, into the crazy asshole and the last one hit home, point blank between his eyes. Miller walked away, getting back into his car.

They pulled away into the night, the cold, destroyed shell of the creep lying empty on the deserted highway. It was over – finally.

Martin Eastland was first published in 2019, and his work has, since, regularly appeared in various anthologies. His debut solo anthology, OUT OF THE ASHES, is available at all online bookstores on January 29, 2024, on ebook and Paperback.

You can find him on X, Instagram, and Facebook by searching 'Martin Eastland'.

GPS

By Justin Sexton

I used Google maps today

Yet somehow I ended up dead on the highway

I did exactly what she asked

But technology failed in my grasp

I took a left and then a right

And ended up lost at night

I should have known all along

That GPS sucks and is usually wrong

Justin Sexton is an author, musician, and podcaster living in the mountains of north Georgia. He finds inspiration for his work in folklore, old-school horror movies, life experiences, and nature.

He currently has a novella "The Nomad" out and another novella "Mirror Island" coming out summer 2024 through Above the Rain Collective.

Acknowledgments

Thank you to all the authors who submitted a story or poem for this anthology. I thoroughly enjoyed working with all of you and getting to know you through your work.

Also much gratitude to Bee, sillyclub.xyz, who did the story art and who originally told me about taxi drivers in Japan with disappearing/ghost passengers which inspired this anthology.

Thank you to our readers. Without you, the story is not finished. You are so appreciated!

Please check us out at:

abovetheraincollective.com